I0731223

HALO ROBERTS

Finding My Sun

A Bit of a Love Rhombus...Is That a Thing?

First edition

ISBN: 978-1-953204-01-1

Cover art by Teshia Saunders
Editing by Taming The Ink

This book was professionally typeset on Reedsy.
Find out more at reedsy.com

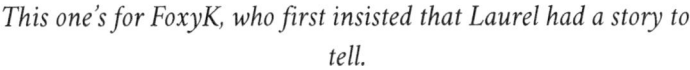

This one's for FoxyK, who first insisted that Laurel had a story to tell.
You were right, Lady, and I thank you.

On an island in the sun
We'll be playing and having fun
And it makes me feel so fine
I can't control my brain

-Weezer

Contents

II   Part Two: A Beach Wedding

I

Part One: A Wink and a Smile

I'm Not Drunk, You're Drunk

*L*aurel

"Macie Moo, I lovvvve you," I hear my own voice over the pounding music and cringe, realizing the whiskey has taken over. Declaring how I feel for this man that is currently holding me up seems like the plan. Leaning back, it's clear that I would tip over if his arm wasn't around me, and I look into his eyes. *Instant regret.*

"You're smashed, Laurel," Mace's beautiful accent rolls over my skin. *It's honestly probably the thing about him that I do love.* His expression is wary. I don't know why I just told him I love him, actually. Seems like a thing to do. So does getting another drink, but he frowns and keeps ahold of me when I try to head for the bar.

Mace Carson, lean, inked, broody. He's a British rock star and he wants everyone to know it, *and I just called him Macie Moo and dropped an L-bomb. Shoot me now.* His eyes flicker over

3

my shoulder, he waves a hand, and one of his security detail appear in my line of sight.

"She's making an idiot of herself, make sure she gets home," Mace extricates himself from my arms, "there's a good girl," he pats me on the ass and nods at his paid gorilla.

"Sure, Boss." The gorilla, I eventually recognize as Tim, gently takes my arm. I've taken two wobbly steps before my slushy brain can send a signal to my mouth.

"Wait, what the hell? Did I just get sent home? Are you fucking kidding me?" As I build up steam, Tim smoothly winds an arm around my waist. Literally picking me up, he carries me to the exit of the club. I'm too shocked to do much more than smack his head and shoulders with my phone. *How in hell have I not lost this thing yet?* Tim's an old pro though, he doesn't stop moving until we reach a sleek black car and he deposits me in the back seat.

"You'll thank me tomorrow, Miss Laurel," he grins and then politely ignores me while I pout in the back seat the entire drive. Pulling up to the entrance of my apartment building, Tim gets out and opens my door, offering me a hand and smoothly passing me on to the doorman. Job done, he gets back in the car and leaves.

"Hello, Ron." I gather the wilted shreds of my dignity about me and wish I'd had the foresight to take off, and carry, my heels. The car ride gave me a moment to sober up a tad and I feel like an ass.

"Evening, Miss Williams, do you need a hand upstairs?" He's trying to hide a smile and I'm grateful.

"No thank you, Ron, I'm fine," I prove it by walking steadily to the elevator and pushing the button. Stepping inside, I wait for the doors to close and rest my forehead on the cool metal panel above the buttons.

This isn't me.

Coffee As Art

〜෴〜

*L*aurel
   3 months later

Humming to myself, I juggle two coffees as I let myself into Mace's penthouse and kick off my shoes. Setting them on the counter, I blink as I see the lineup of empty bottles on the counter. *Somebody had a hell of a night.* It's not uncommon, just a little unusual for a Tuesday.

Ever since my embarrassing ride home, I've stepped back from the endless parties that swept me away when Mace and I started dating. Mace and I have realized that we connect on a deeper level. We've been exploring our relationship as he works on his next album. *I'm totally taking credit for that, I'm his muse.* We've slowed things down, *way...way down,* because Mace wants to concentrate on his music, and I've strictly avoided any repeats of the L-word.

The words are just flowing as Mace writes his new songs. It

takes up all of his time, it's become his obsession. He's clearly inspired and his bandmates are anxious to get in the studio and start recording. *Probably the reason for all the bottles, they must have finally had a session last night.*

All of this time for thought and reflection has been good for me. *I keep telling myself that, otherwise I've just been doing a lot of yoga and trying not to die of boredom.*

I've started writing again too, resurrecting the blog that I began a few years ago while travelling with my father, I want to share it with Mace. I feel like it's time for him to start sharing in the things I'm interested in, branching out. I'd like him to travel with me, explore some new places. I'm nervous about bringing it up, but we care about each other, we need to keep growing together.

Leaving my bag on the counter, I pick up the coffees, crossing the living area as I head for the bedroom. Mace is probably still sleeping. As I walk down the hall, my feet sink into plush carpet, making no sound. Mace and I both startle as we meet at his bedroom door.

"Laurel, shit! Startled me Love!" Mace whispers, stepping into the hall and pulling the door shut behind him. *Weird.* He's got a shirt in his hand and he quickly pulls it over his head, running a hand through his hair.

"Hey, good morning," I tilt my head up and lean in to give him a kiss. He gives me the most perfunctory of pecks. *Weird.* He gingerly takes one of the coffees out of my hand.

"Cheers, Love, this is perfect, let's go sit by the pool," he takes my arm to steer me back out to the living room. *Weird, weird, weird.*

"You know what? I think you're acting weird, so I'd like to see what's behind door number one first." Pulling my elbow out of his grasp, I quickly turn the doorknob and push the door open. Mace steps in my line of sight, but not before I see a flash of black hair as someone disappears into the bathroom.

"Laurel, you don't-" Mace falters as I turn to him, but whatever my face is doing must be pretty fierce because he just gets out of my way. Stomping into the room, I raise my hand to knock on the bathroom door. It flies open before my knuckles make contact and I gasp.

"Gabs? What the? Why are you-?" I'm so confused to see her standing there, her brown eyes swimming with tears. *She's wearing Mace's robe. Why is she wearing Mace's robe?*

"I'm so sorry," she whispers, "I didn't want you to find out this way, we made a mistake..." Gabrielle flaps her hands helplessly as I stand there speechless. "Please, Laurel, can we-" she bites her lip, shaking her head as tears start to slide down her cheeks.

"Laurel, Love," Mace is trying for a soothing tone. "Let's go talk." Turning to look at him, I feel a smile stretching my lips. I back away from his outstretched hand, shaking my head slowly.

"Hmmm, that's a pass." Realizing I'm still holding my coffee, I take a sip. "Well shoot, it's gone cold." I whisper, and then before I can think too hard, I turn and throw it as hard as I can at the wall. It explodes, a beautiful splatter appearing on the white wool of the upholstered headboard, dripping down to soak the bedding. Gabs lets out a startled shriek. Mace is silent.

Nodding politely at each of them, I walk out of the room. I can feel their eyes on my back.

"Oh Laurel, I'm so sorry," I hear Gabrielle whisper my name sadly.

I've never been as damn proud of myself as I am right now.

8

I don't scream at them and I will never let them see me cry. *Two-timing, faithless, wankers, they can have each other.* I simply put on my shoes, grab my bag and walk away from my new ex…and my new ex-best friend.

The Age of Laurel

L aurel

The flights are long. I've got two layovers to change my mind and go back, but I don't. There's really no elegant way to phrase it, I'm running away. The city has nothing I want right now. I'm feeling lost and alone and I need to regroup.

As I sip a new coffee in the Chicago airport during my first layover, my mind wanders to Gabrielle. My heart hurts and my chest feels like it's caving in, *how could she do this to us?* We've been friends since primary school. I can't remember life before Gabs. I'll never forget the day we met.

It was an average fall morning, rapidly going to crap for me, because a boy in our class decided to make fun of my freckles. The super-unfortunate nickname 'Poop-sprinkles' was just starting to gain some traction when Gabrielle came on the scene. She's always been impulsive with a quick temper. A bloody nose for him, a black eye for her and a call to both of their parents later, we were best friends.

Camps, riding lessons, cheerleading, we were inseparable. We double dated, smoked for the first time, got drunk on my Nana's peach schnapps...it was always Gabs and Laurel. There were times, sure, college and after, that we weren't as close, especially when she studied abroad. Somehow we have always managed to have one of those friendships that just picks up right where it left off.

Wiping a tear off my cheek, I toss my coffee cup in a bin and head for my gate. The unfortunate thing between Gabrielle and I is that *she* was the one who made friends easily. I never had any problem finding a date, and I had a small, *very small* circle of friends, but most of them I met through Gabrielle. She's just one of those people that has a little magic.

I was the shy one, the bookish one, the girl who always had to force myself to get out there and be social when what I *really* wanted was yoga pants, a pint of ice cream and a *Vampire Diaries* marathon. I, finally, *this sounds so lame,* 'found myself' in college, discovered how much I love to write, and how exciting it was when I had early success with a number of freelance articles.

Gabrielle was always there, cheering me on, helping me curse the editors that I butted heads with, showing up with a bottle of wine and a smile when she knew I needed it most. I hadn't realized until now that I relied on her for so much of my confidence. The betrayal cuts deep, and it's my Gabs that I'm losing.

Mace and I were new. When I think of him, I just feel stupid. We met at a party and he intrigued me. I thought I wanted to be a rockstar's girlfriend. *I hope he gets a rash...and fleas...and a sunburn.*

The layover is long and I've got nothing but time to think about my life. I think about the city, my life there, the dreams I had when I first moved into my own apartment, *all ready to adult the hell out of life.* It's easy to see now that I was falling into a rut of my own making, lazy and comfortable. I took everything for granted, nothing changed...*until everything did.*

Enough. I'm not going to feel sorry for myself. I'm not going to wallow. I'm *certainly* not going to look back and have any regrets. What I *am* going to do is start living for myself. I'm going to be happy. I'm going to do, and create, things that bring me joy. I'm going to have people in my life that make me want to be better, to do more, to love harder. *I am going to be the brightest goddamn ray of sunshine ever.*

As the attendant calls for boarding, I square my shoulders and march down the jetway. It's time for me to get on with my own life. It's time for me to stop relying on other people to make me happy. It is the age of Laurel.

The flight attendant's face when I marched on the plane, loudly humming The Age of Aquarius, was the best thing that has happened to me all year.

I Need a Hug

L *aurel*

"Hi Dad." I've done so well up until right this second, but now my eyes brim up and spill over without warning as I drop my bags and dive into his arms.

"Laurel?" He crushes me to him, letting me stain the front of his shirt with tears.

"Laurel?" A feminine voice echoes, and I look up to see Margo walk out of the kitchen, drying her hands. Tossing the towel on the bar, she doesn't miss a beat as she finishes off the hug-sandwich. We just stand there, no words needed, and I feel better already.

When they finally step back, Dad doesn't let go of my shoulders as he looks me over carefully. His stern face is serious as he meets my eyes.

"What happened?" He says quietly, and tears threaten again, but I manage to blink them away.

"Oh…my love life is in shambles…" my voice is wobbly as I try a smile. "You can say 'I told you so' about Mace if you want to, Dad." He smiles briefly but it doesn't reach his eyes.

"I don't like to be correct if it causes you sorrow, Laurel," he smooths my hair, "do you want to…tell me about it?" I can't help a tiny laugh at the pause in his question, *yes Dad, I'd like to tell you all about my feelings, welcome to Hell.*

I love him for the offer. There have been many years of my life where I unloaded whatever drama was bothering me on my patient father. He's always listened, offering sage advice *that often sounds suspiciously like it's been plagiarized from The Art of War, which I think might be his manual for dealing with people, and adjusted to fit the particular circumstances.* Margo links an arm through mine.

"Girl talk, Babe," she winks at him and pulls me towards the bar. "Let's grab a drink, Chica, then you tell me all about it." I hide a smile at the relieved look on his face. I can't even begin to explain how grateful I am that my dad found Margo. He'd probably be surprised to find out that I've long suspected he has Asperger's. She just absolutely gets him, they're amazing together.

My dad and Margo eloped several years ago and bought a bar on a tiny Caribbean island. He had to make several trips back home to tie up loose ends, so this is my first visit. Glancing around, I can see why they fell in love with this place.

A dark teak bar dominates the back of the room, tables dot the floor with cheerful tablecloths fluttering in the breeze. It's what the bar faces that is the most amazing thing. Large wooden shutters on tracks slide back to open the entire wall of the bar to the ocean. A large deck continues the space, a woven roof providing shade. Underneath, twinkle lights and colorful lanterns hang, waiting for the evening. Beyond the deck, white sand and clear blue water as far as the eye can see.

"If you need some heart-healing, the islands are the place to be," Margo smiles, as she deposits me on a bar stool and walks around the bar to face me. Dad gives me a big hug from behind, kissing the top of my head.

"This bar in particular," he hugs me again, "Margo's sangria will make you sing, and I'm quite adept in the kitchen. I'm going to prepare for you what Margo will only refer to as 'belly magic,'" he pauses, and I look up over my shoulder. It surprises me to see a look of anger mixed with dark humor on his face as he continues.

"I will rely on you and Margo to determine if there is any sort of vengeful fatherly duty required now that Mace has caused you to have hurt feelings. I will operate under the assumption that the blame rests solely on his shoulders. Just say the word, my darlings." I laugh softly and he pats my back, drops another kiss on my head and disappears through the swinging door behind the bar to the kitchen. Margo watches him leave, smiling fondly, before turning back to me.

"He's serious, you know," Margo chuckles, "but he does have a code of honor." Reaching up, she pulls down a glass, wiping it with a soft towel. "*I*, however, do not. If that jackass deserves it, I will hunt him down, bury him up to his neck in a tidal pool and hand him a long curly straw." She smiles evilly and gives me a wink as I burst into startled giggles at *that* mental picture. It feels so good to be here, knowing I've got them in my corner. I feel tears threaten again and blink hard.

"You're in for a treat, Chica," Margo sets the glass in front of me and reaches into the fridge behind the bar. Pulling out a pitcher, she carefully pours me a glass of sangria and uses a spoon to add some of the fruit. I take a sip and hum appreciatively.

"Hmmm well *that's* freaking delicious."

"Oh, wait until you get a bite of your dad's cooking," Margo smiles at my assessment and pours herself a glass. She takes a sip and eyes me over the rim.

I don't even know where to start, it's just a lot, and my eyes fill with tears. Dashing them away angrily, I turn on my stool and look at the ocean.

"Come on Chica," Margo murmurs, pretending not to notice as I wipe away a few escapee tears with the back of my hand. She picks up her drink and heads for the deck, walking out to the edge and sinking onto a comfortable couch covered in tropical print. I follow suit and we sit in silence for a moment, staring at the waves crashing on the beach.

"Your dad didn't want to be right about Mace, you know," Margo says quietly, still staring at the waves, "he worries about you, he misses you more than you know." She glances at me and then pretends to be interested in fishing a berry out of her glass with a little plastic cocktail sword.

"It wasn't just Mace," I sigh, running a finger aimlessly around the rim of my glass, "it was…Gabs too…" I don't want to say it out loud. I don't want to think about what would make my best friend decide a man should come between us, I don't even know the answer. I look at Margo and her eyes are wide.

"What did Gabrielle do?" As soon as Margo says the words, it all clicks and she gasps. "You are fucking *joking*, Chica. No, don't even, ohmygod, okay, tell me." She waves her hands at herself in a 'bring it on' motion and I blurt out a laugh full of tears.

"Yeah, Gabs and Mace slept together…she was still there

when I showed up with coffee." An embarrassed little sob sneaks out and I look away again, taking another drink.

"Oh Chica, *please* tell me you ran over one or both of them with your car," Margo fumes helplessly, setting her glass on the table next to her with a hard clink.

"Where are you at in your mad, honey?" Margo stands, pacing in front of me, "I'll catch up, do you need to cry a little? I've got a shoulder. Curse them both? I'll teach you some new words and whip up a voodoo doll. Drink a gallon of sangria? I'll pour all night. I got you Chica." She holds out both hands and when I take them, Margo pulls me up with surprising enthusiasm, straight into a hug.

"Just keep me the hell away from my phone, especially if I've had a lot of this sangria…and some more sangria would be really nice," my voice is muffled in her shoulder, but the hug is everything I needed right now. I'm not alone. Everything will be okay.

On With Life

*L*aurel

Waking up to the distant sound of the waves and the birds calling, I stretch luxuriously. My dad and Margo live just beyond the outskirts of town, in a sprawling bungalow built into the side of the hills overlooking the beach. Open to the ocean breeze, a fan swirls lazily over my head and I can almost taste the salt in the air.

The shattered feeling I had in my chest is still there, little shards of sadness and doubt lodged around my heart. Out of habit, I glance at my phone on the bedside table. I've got 36 missed call notifications, all from Gabs. One text from Mace.

Mace: sorry Love

Wow. That's deep and heartfelt. Rolling my eyes so hard I'm in actual danger of falling off the bed, I toss my phone aside.

I wasn't even going to look at it for a while, I wish I hadn't bothered. I'd love to go back to sleep and forget it all, but I don't think that will work.

Climbing out of bed with a sigh, I dig around in my bags. Liberally smearing my entire self with sunscreen, I pull on a bikini and t-shirt dress. After a glance in the mirror, I gather my hair up into a messy bun. The humidity here is a force to be reckoned with, and my hair is something of a beast in the best of conditions. Long and fiery red, *thanks Mom,* it *usually* falls down my back in relaxed waves that stop just shy of becoming real curls. Here, every piece along my hairline has become a little corkscrew. It's so fluffy the bun is damn near the same size as my head.

Stepping into some sandals and grabbing my sunglasses, I walk out onto the deck off my bedroom. Stretching the length of the house, all of the rooms are open to the deck. My father is sitting at a small table just outside the kitchen, sipping coffee and staring at the ocean.

"I heard you moving around, I thought you might like some breakfast," he stands with a smile, walking over to meet me before leading me to the other chair at the table. Fresh fruit and granola wait in bowls, the tantalizing smell of coffee drifts up to tease me.

"Good thought, yes," I hug him before sitting, reaching for the coffee, "I wish I'd come sooner, this place is amazing."

"It is indeed," he returns to his own chair, reaching for the granola. "I wish you hadn't come under the circumstances that you are unhappy, but I am very glad to see you nonetheless." His words make me smile, I've missed his eloquent speech patterns. My father always sounds so formal, but he's really not at all. We eat in companionable silence for a few moments.

"I've resurrected my blog," I begin, not wanting to talk about Mace or Gabs. From the look of relief that flits across his face, he didn't either. Margo and I hashed everything out enough last night. Now I just want all the pieces in my chest to line up and come together again.

"That is good news indeed, Laurel," my dad has alway enjoyed reading articles I write and following my blog. "Did you bring your camera? There is much to be documented here on the island."

"I did," I nod, words muffled around a mouthful of fruit. Pausing to swallow, I contemplate my next words.

Dad and I traveled extensively a few of years ago, just before he met Margo. I documented our trips obsessively, it was one of the happiest times of my life. He took great joy in seeing the photographs and words put together. I knew he was disappointed when I set it aside for the more lucrative freelance work I had started to score on a regular basis.

I think he was trying to lure me back into it a year or so ago when he had me take over the website management for the gallery he is a partial owner of back in the city. He's a happily silent partner now, he calls it early retirement. I've always been proficient with tech, a degree in print marketing didn't hurt anything. *I mostly used the emphasis in photography to turn my hobby into an obsession.* Even so, I'm a quite highly paid webmaster...suspiciously so, but it's always been Dad's way to take care of me on the sly.

"I believe I'm done living in the city for a time, Dad," I glance at him to see his reaction, but other than watching me steadily, he's just waiting for me to continue.

"I want to pick up where we left off, keep writing, keep trav-

20

elling," I shrug helplessly, "the city just doesn't have anything for me, I don't know why I stayed when you left, I can write anywhere. I don't need to physically go in and meet with editorial anymore…" Popping a piece of mango in my mouth, I stare at the water.

"I believe that this is a wise decision." My father says seriously, taking another drink of his coffee before he continues. "I have long hoped that you would find a way to give yourself freedom, release yourself from the confines of the concrete jungle." He smiles at me. "Margo is fond of reminding me that our story will at some point read, 'The End'. Let's make sure we get all the living done first, hmm?"

I Spy With My Little Eye

Laurel

The sand is warm and soft under my feet as I wander along the beach. This isn't one of the busier islands. There's a cute little market in the center of town, a couple of other restaurants along with Margo's and quiet beaches. A large flat rock looms up out of the sand, just far enough back that the water isn't reaching it at this point in the day. I climb up and sit on top of it, enjoying the morning breeze.

Gulls comb the beach, their high-pitched calls sounding like laughter as they investigate everything that washes in, hopping around on the sand and then taking to the air. The waves are fierce and beautiful, the crash and boom of the surf is followed by the rattle of small rocks being dragged over each other by the power of the water. Some of the tiny bays dotting the cliffs to either side of the beach are covered in smooth black rocks, rather than sand. As a particularly large wave crests, I see a man surfing.

I know nothing about surfing, but I can tell he's good…very, very good. He looks super relaxed, but as I lift up my camera to get a better look, I can see the definition in every muscle as he leans. I lose sight of him for a moment as he disappears under a curl of water. He reappears, leaning and dragging his fingers along the perfect wall of water at his back as he flies across the wave. I quickly take a few pictures before he lazily topples into the water. He surfaces and flips his dark hair back before he climbs on his board and starts paddling back out.

I'm glued to the rock, mesmerized by the raw beauty of the ocean and the way it's being mastered. Over and over he rides the waves, until finally he strides to the shore. Water glistens on every muscle. His shoulders are broad, his hips are narrow, every inch of him is lean, muscular perfection. *Down girl, holy crap, this is stalker level eye-banging.* All of a sudden I feel weird. *Hi Hot Surfer Guy, don't mind me, I'm just the creeper on the rock taking pictures.*

I don't think he's seen me yet, so I do what makes the most sense under the circumstances. I jump off the rock and hide behind it. *Ohmygod what if he already saw me, what the hell am I doing hiding behind a rock?* Quickly putting my camera in my bag, I shoulder it and decide to walk back to the house as if I didn't just hide like a weirdo.

I wait until I'm almost at the edge of my dad's deck before risking a look back. *Yep, Hot Surfer Guy is most definitely standing where I last saw him, watching me walk away. I wonder if he lives here? Probably running away like a scared rabbit was not the best way to find out. Sigh.*

Dad and Margo aren't home. A note is pinned under a large seashell on the table.

Hey Chica, hope you had a good walk. Nothing like ocean air and warm sand. We are at the bar, come on over later and have dinner. No rush. Use the minibike if you like.

Margo

I take a couple of hours, clear up some emails and write my next blog post, including some photos of the amazing waves I watched crash the beach this morning. I don't want to forget any of the details, the sounds and feelings. I can still smell the salt in my hair.

Finally, setting my laptop aside, I shower quickly, loosely braiding my hair to keep it under control. Dressing in flowy linen trousers and a thin blue tee with a deep v-neck, I look at my camera lying on the bed and pick it up.

Scrolling back through the pictures I took of the surfer, I zoom in to look at him again. Dark bronze skin, every muscle taut as he leans into the curve of a wave. *I'd sell a lesser-used body part for skin like that, I bet he never burns.* Dark hair, longer on top that he flips out of his eyes in a practiced movement every time he surfaces. His eyes are a surprising bright blue.

My stomach growls hungrily, pulling my attention away from the surfer's blue eyes. I'm excited for more of Dad's cooking. Last night was literally the best thing I've ever eaten in my life. Leaving my camera on the bed, I glance in the mirror, roll my eyes at the curls already escaping my braid and walk out of the house.

I smile with delight as I see the little motorbike Margo mentioned in a carport off the back of the house. My dad and I spent many of our travels renting these to buzz around and see the sights. This one is downright adorable, mint green with a white metal basket on the front. A matching moto helmet sits on the seat. The car is still parked nearby, so Margo and Dad must have doubled up. Stowing my bag in the basket, I put on the helmet and take a leisurely ride to Margo's.

The Redhead on the Rock

*T*rey

I wasn't expecting to see anyone on the beach today.

I was surfing, just messing around, having fun, when I saw her perched on a rock. It was like the mermaid from that Disney movie, brought to life. She looked beautiful, pale skin, masses of red hair. I kept surfing for a while, showing off.

When I walked in, planning to talk to her, she quickly left the beach before I got close enough to say hello. It actually looked like she was *hiding* for a second, but maybe she's shy. She *did* give me a little glance back though, just a peek over her shoulder, before she went in the house.

My house is at the other end of the beach, tucked back into some trees that jut out into the sand. It's quiet here, but the silence is broken by a familiar yowl.

"Hey Ollie," I greet the cat that shimmies out from the shade under the deck to wrap around my legs. She lets out another yowl and head butts my calf. I lean down and scratch between her ears before she puts her claws to my leg to get my attention. I stow my board on the rack near the deck and Ollie follows me into the house.

Filling Ollie's food bowl, I lean against the counter, thinking about the woman on the beach. She must have arrived pretty recently, I would have noticed someone in town with hair that color. It's a small island, one of the quieter ones, no resorts or cruise ship ports. Here it's just friendly locals, a busy marketplace, a couple of good bars and a trickle of tourism from the next island over that has a resort.

Grabbing my phone, I ignore the calls from my agent, he's working on some endorsement deal that I don't care about that much, I'll call him later. I swipe open the texts from my friend Brian, I've missed several while I was surfing.

B: Dude where u at?
   B: final weekend before circuit training let's do it up
   B: …
   B: u surfin without me chump?
   B: …
   B: call me let's meet up this weekend
   B: later

Final weekend before circuit training, which is always brutal. It's all self-inflicted though, Brian and I have been pushing each other for years. He's got a house the next island over. He likes to be where the action is, spends a few months a year there. We run the circuit together and he has another house in Florida.

T: weekend sounds good holler at you later

Walking through the kitchen and down a short hall to the bedroom, I toss my phone on the bed and head for the shower. I've got a redhead to meet.

Twenty-Six Minutes to Heaven

L aurel

"Did you have a relaxing afternoon, Chica?" Margo sets a glass of sangria down in front of me and leans a hip on the edge of the table.

"I did," I smile, taking a sip of sangria, "I managed to smear on enough spf 90 to avoid a sunburn and took a ton of great photos." I hold out an arm to prove my lack of crispiness. Margo laughs.

"Babe, are you cooking for Laurel or do you want me to have Jay whip something up tonight?" Margo turns to Dad, who stands quickly.

"Give me twenty-six minutes," he says with a quick smile, heading to the kitchen. Margo nods at a man at a table nearby who is trying to get her attention, and I realize the bar is getting busier by the minute.

"Is it always this crowded?" All of the tables are full, and there are a number of people at the bar.

"Oh, this is pretty normal for a Thursday night," Margo nods, "it just feels busier because one of my waitresses quit on me. Get this, her *horoscope* told her to quit, supposedly 'destiny' is going to drop a millionaire in her lap sometime this month." Margo snorts and rolls her eyes and I laugh.

"Is there anything I can do to help?"

"Enjoy your dinner first, Chica, but after that, I wouldn't say no if you wanted to run a few drinks out for me." Margo smiles and pats my shoulder, moving towards the next table.

Sipping my sangria, I stare out at the beach, enjoying the sunset. Of course my mind wanders right back to Hot Surfer Guy. I wonder if he ever comes here to eat. *If he doesn't it would be my civic duty to tell him about the food...maybe I could offer to be the plate...ohmygod that's weird.*

My musing is delightfully interrupted by a large bowl of gumbo and a small plate of cornbread. I sigh with true happiness as I smell the food, and my father smiles, sitting down with his own plate.

"How is it that I missed out on this level of cuisine growing up?" I tease, and he barks out a laugh.

"If I had dared to put that plate in front of 10-year-old Laurel, I would have been accused of poisoning my child," he smiles, "*you*, my darling, were the *pickiest* of eaters."

"Oh I wasn't *that* bad," I poke back, words muffled by the food I can't stop shovelling in my mouth.

"No?" He feigns shock, "You subsisted *strictly* on boxed macaroni and cheese, liberally slathered with *ketchup* of all things." I burst out laughing as he shudders, a look of disgust on his face. "Not to mention a devotion to those horrible little packaged brownies that bordered on religious fervor. If that does not qualify as picky, I'm not sure what does." He taps his chin reflectively. "As I think back on it, the only real question is how you ever discovered either of those things, *I refuse to call them food*, in the first place?"

"What happened at Nana's *stays* at Nana's," I try to look prim, but fail and laugh, lifting my sangria in a toast. He laughs with me and clinks the rim of his glass to mine.

Dinner at Margo's

Trey

I walk up on the deck at Margo's bar and sit at my usual table. It's near the edge of the deck, out of the way. I like to people-watch, and the food is ridiculously good. I know Margo lives in the house that the red-head walked into, I wonder how they're related. *I also wonder if the red-head is single and if Margo will introduce me.*

Margo's man is sitting at a small table that's always reserved for him, a glass of whiskey glowing in the evening light beside his book. He gives me a nod and continues reading. I'm not sure what his name is, she always calls him 'Babe'. He leaves most of the talking to Margo, his sun rises and sets with that woman. He's got her and he takes over the kitchen on those magical nights when the mood strikes him, turning out food better than any I've ever had in my life. Otherwise, he can usually be found, chilling, with a book and a drink.

Later in the evenings, the music gets a little louder, and sometimes I stay at my table, watching the crowd. I've discovered that at the end of each night, he carefully places a bookmark, stands up from the table, finds Margo wherever she is in the bar, and they dance.

"Evening, Trey," Margo smiles at me, balancing a full tray on one hand as she pauses by my table. "Dinner and a beer?"

"Yes, please," I never order anything specific, Margo just brings me a plate. The bar is busy tonight. There's no band, but one of the line cooks likes to set up playlists on the off nights. As soon as he starts up the music, several couples hit the floor. The mood is high, everyone having a good time, laughing and drinking.

And just like magic, there she is, the redhead from the beach. Gracefully winding her way through the tables, she's delivering drinks and smiles. I can occasionally hear her soft voice as she chats with customers. She lifts her head when the bartender calls her over to the bar, going back for another round to deliver.

Margo drops off my beer as she walks by and then pauses, following my gaze.

"That's Babe's daughter Laurel," Margo says quietly. "She left a lot of drama in the city. She could use a friend." She moves away from my table, already chatting with someone else.

Laurel. She's probably just helping out tonight because the bar is so busy, one of the usual waitresses is missing. I wonder what drama she left behind. I wonder if she's staying a while. *I wonder if she'd dance with me.*

As I'm staring at the ocean, drinking my beer and daydreaming, I feel a soft touch on my shoulder. I turn to look and she's there, a small smile quirking up the corner of her mouth. Her eyes are a dark soulful brown. She's got a dimple.

"Sorry if I startled you, it's kind of crowded and the plate's hot," her voice is soft and musical. As our eyes meet, she looks at me a little harder and I see a blush staining her cheeks pink. *Yep, I'm the surfer from earlier, nice to meet you beautiful. Will you marry me? Probably too soon.*

"Um, can I bring you anything else?" I realize I'm just sitting there mentally proposing, *so I also mentally punch myself in the face. Talk to her, you idiot.*

"This looks great," when I finally speak she nods her head, job done, starting to turn away. *No, no, no, keep her talking.*

"I'm Trey," I toss out quickly. Her eyes meet mine again and her smile lights up my world.

"Laurel, nice to meet you, Trey." We shake hands, her skin is smooth, a pale cream. A few freckles scattered across the back of her hand match the dusting of tinier freckles across her nose. *Okay, Brain, now what?*

"Do you come here often?" As soon as the words leave my mouth, she laughs and I can't help but join her. *So lame. You're fired, Brain.*

"Well my first day on the island was yesterday, so not really," she tilts her head, still amused.

"That was lame," I reach for my beer almost desperately.

"That *was* lame," she agrees, "but if you meant am I *new in town*," she wiggles her eyebrows, acknowledging the joke, "yes. I'm here visiting my dad and his wife, they own this place." We both look towards the bar as I hear Margo call for Laurel.

"That's my cue," Laurel says softly, "it was nice to meet you, Trey."

"Can I see you again?"

Her eyes widen and she nods shyly.

"I'll be at the beach tomorrow morning." She turns and walks towards the bar. *Come on, Beautiful, give me a look back.*

Just before she disappears in the crowd on the dance floor, Laurel looks back and gives me a little wink. Smiling, I eat my dinner and finish my beer. Tossing Margo a wave, I step off the deck and head home across the beach.

Meet Me at the Beach

*L*aurel

The rest of the night is a blur. It felt so good to feel *seen*. Trey is hot, *like, fan yourself and giggle like an idiot hot.* My battered ego needed the attention. The angry-at-Mace side of me keeps piping in, reminding me I don't need a man to be happy. *Totally true, of course, but that doesn't mean I'm not interested.* Would it be so bad to have some fun?

I remind myself sternly about my decision at the airport. This is The Age of Laurel. I don't need just any man, I want someone to share things with, someone who makes me feel special. I want someone who lets me be strong and silly and grouchy *and doesn't make me apologize for being an emotional wreck when they roll out the Christmas movies on Hallmark every year.*

I want someone who lights a fire under me so hot that a little grin melts my underpants. A look across the room puts a quiver in my belly. A touch raises goosebumps *everywhere.* I don't know if Trey is all of those things, but he's off to a hell of a start.

* * *

I'm awake ridiculously early. *Especially* early when you consider how long it took me to go to sleep last night. What kept me tossing and turning into the wee hours was my absolute, instant and utter attraction to Trey. It was all I could do last night to walk away. I couldn't leave without looking back and tossing him a wink. After I did, I felt ridiculously brave.

I'm *never* the one to initiate a chase when it comes to men. Imagine my surprise when that wink felt like child's play. *What I really wanted to do was climb in his lap, steal a sip of his beer, and kiss the daylights out of him.* Maybe I should have.

I've just barely walked away from Mace. Am I rebounding? Am I looking for someone to reassure me? Make me feel desirable? Someone to make me forget that my ex-boyfriend chose my best friend over me *and she let him?*

Maybe.

There's something about Trey though…this doesn't feel like a rebound. When I was talking to him last night for those brief moments, there was nothing further from my mind than Mace and Gabs.

Giving up any pretense of sleeping, I toss back the covers with a sigh and pull on a bikini, covering it with a lace sundress. Wandering out to the deck, I look down the way. My father is sitting in his usual seat at the table, flipping through a newspaper. I smile as I notice two steaming cups of espresso sending a delicious scent my way from their place on the table. *I'm not even going to pretend to guess how he always times that right.*

"Good morning, Daughter." As I walk to the table, he carefully folds his newspaper and moves one of the cups closer to an empty chair. I smile at the familiar formality of his greeting, and adopt an uppity tone that brings a matching smile to his face.

"Good m-ah-ning Fah-thah," I drop a quick curtsy before I take my seat and he barks out a laugh.

"Margo has much to say about my inability to adopt what she calls, 'island vibes'," Dad muses, "it is not in my nature to adopt local customs and speech patterns," he pauses, taking a drink of espresso, "I have long been more an observer of human interactions."

"A very *astute* observer," Margo chimes in, coming from the kitchen and stopping to give my dad a quick kiss, "and I wouldn't change a word you say, Babe." She pats my shoulder and takes a seat at the table with us, a large mug of coffee, with so much cream in it that it's beige, in her hands. "So, Chica, what's on the agenda for today?" She smiles, sipping her 'coffee' as she watches me over the rim.

"*Well*…I met a guy at the bar last night, Trey. We made kind of loose plans to meet at the beach today." I busy myself sipping espresso, a hated blush pinking up my cheeks.

"Oh that sounds fun, he's a sweetie," Margo smiles. "It never hurts to meet some of the other 'fish in the sea', Chica."

"Also, I had fun last night waiting tables, I'd be happy to cover more evenings until you find a new waitress, I'd like to help."

I'd like to have less time to sit and mope. *Maybe Trey can help with that too...*

"Of course! I'll even show you my super-duper top secret Sangria recipe," Margo smiles and winks.

* * *

Shoving my camera, sandals and an ever-necessary bottle of sunscreen in a small backpack, I put on a large pair of sunglasses and wave goodbye to Margo. The sun is warm but there's a gentle breeze that keeps the heat from being oppressive and the sand is so soft. I meander along the quiet stretch of beach where I first saw Trey. He's standing at the edge of the ocean, gazing out at the waves. He turns, smiling when he sees me and I sketch a little wave.

I admire his easy strength, *and wish I had my camera out,* when he jogs over to meet me. Slowing a few feet away, his blue eyes look relieved as he grins, teeth a bright white against his skin. *Oomph, I felt that grin ping me right in the hoo-ha.*

"I'm glad you came," his deep voice sends another jolt, and I'm starting to wonder if the oxygen content of the air is different in the islands, because I feel light-headed. *For fuckssake pull yourself together Laurel, stop with the horny thoughts...seriously, stop. Okay one more... No! Just kidding, stop.* Resisting the urge to fan myself, I smile back. *Okay, good. Smiling, good.*

"So, I was wondering if maybe you wanted to see more of the island today?" Trey continues when I don't fill the silence, *because I'm an idiot, desperately begging my brain and mouth to come together and cooperate.*

"I'd like that." *Oh thank god.*

A Jump and a Kiss

*T*rey

Hanging out with Laurel is effortless. She lets me help her with a helmet, ties her skirt in a knot with a laugh and climbs on the bike behind me. Her arms slide around my waist lightly, tightening as we pick up a little speed. Her body is warm against my back.

We ride all over the island. I show her the fort that was the original town center back in the 1800's, we walk the cliffs on the far side of the island and make our way to the market in the center of town.

"Ok, Girl, hand it over," Laurel brought a camera with her and she takes pictures at each place we stop, asking me about history and laughing at my stories of some of the crazier locals. I can tell I'm in a few of the pictures.

"Hand what over?" She looks adorably confused. I hold out my hand for the camera.

"My turn, the sun in your hair needs documenting," I wiggle my fingers, silently asking for the camera again. She blushes and gives it to me, a small smile on her lips. She's sitting at a small table in the market, sipping a mojito. She's beautiful. I take a couple of pictures and hang the camera around my neck, she laughs.

"Actually, when I saw you surfing yesterday I was taking pictures. You know, just first impressions of the beach and the water," Laurel says casually, looking up at me through her lashes. "So, when I saw you surfing I took a few of you too, I hope you don't mind," she adds shyly.

"No, that's cool, I don't mind." At this point, I'm pretty sure Laurel has never heard of me. It feels really good, funnily enough. "Can I see them?" I lift up the camera, about to take the strap off my neck, when she shakes her head.

"No, I can't see them?"

"No, sorry, I meant not on the camera," Laurel smiles, "here, you can look at them on my phone, it downloads automatically, the screen is bigger." She reaches into her bag, pulling out her phone. After a moment, she hands it to me with a picture on the screen.

"Wow," it's not the most amazing comment ever, but it might be the most amazing picture. Laurel managed to catch me just as I left the barrel, fingers trailing in the wall. She's quiet as I start looking through more of the pictures, she got every feature of the beach framed beautifully. I flip back to the pictures she took of me and look at them carefully.

"You're very good," I say, glancing up to catch her eyes. Laurel grins.

"It's not rocket science with that kind of subject matter, but... thank you."

"No really though," I want her to understand, "I've seen pictures of myself surfing before, but the problem is I'm always in a competition or training hard, so I never look like I'm having fun." I flip the phone around so she can see the screen. "This guy looks like he's having fun, that's the best picture of me surfing I've ever seen."

"I'm glad I was there to catch you having fun," Laurel rewards me with a brilliant smile.

* * *

Just before we leave the marketplace, I stop at a small cart pushed by a tiny old woman and buy a large woven flower. The old woman cackles and runs her fingers through a strand of Laurel's hair, shaking her head and marveling at the color before moving on.

Laurel blushes but looks into my eyes as I clip it carefully in her hair just behind her ear. I take another picture of her, and give back the camera.

"You're beautiful," I whisper before Laurel looks away, wishing I could freeze time and just stay right here, looking at her. The pink in her cheeks deepens, but her chin lifts, her lips parting slightly. That tiny movement sends a flash of heat through my chest. I reach for her, one hand sliding around her waist, one bunching up in her hair. I pull her to me almost roughly, lower my head and our lips meet.

She takes a tiny step forward, bringing our bodies even closer together. I feel her hands slide around my waist, fingers light on the muscles of my back as she kisses me back. Laurel's kiss is warm and soft. Her lips part and I feel the flick of her tongue, teasing me, before she draws back breathing faster. Leaning forward, I steal another kiss.

"Come on, there's something else I want to show you." I take her hand and we walk back toward my bike. I swing my leg over and hold the bike steady. I don't know why it feels so good that she just hops on and wraps her arms around my waist like we've been together for years. She snuggles tight against my back, her fingers playing along my ribs.

We ride towards the center of the island. Turning off the highway, I take her on a slow ride further inland. The road narrows until it's really more of a path, cutting through the forest for about a mile. I hear Laurel gasp and I smile as we leave the heavy canopy and come into a tiny clearing.

"The river has kind of a natural bottle neck on the rocks here," I point up beyond a small waterfall as I turn off the bike, holding it steady while Laurel climbs off. There's a wide, shallow river running through the island, clear water lazily weaving through the thick forest.

"There are about a million things here that I want to take pictures of, Trey, this is *beautiful*," she breathes, turning in a full circle to look around.

"We've got all day," I shrug, "we can stay as long as you like." Leaving the bike in the shade, I grab my bag out of the seat and hold out my hand. Laurel takes it and we walk down some natural stairs in the rock.

The waterfall has a small pool that narrows at one end where it goes through some rocks and then widens into a slow moving river again. In the middle of the pool is a large flat rock, big enough for several people to fit on. Stopping near the edge of the pool, I look down at Laurel.

"If we leave our stuff here, we can follow the trail up above the waterfall and then ride the river down." I leave my bag on a dry rock by a tree, pulling off my shirt. Tossing it on my bag, I turn to Laurel and stifle a groan. *This is the best idea I've had in a long time.* She's pulling her dress up over her head, folding it and laying it on her own bag. She carefully unclips the flower from her hair and tucks it under the dress.

Laurel is wearing a pale blue bikini. I caught flashes of the color through the lace of her dress, but I wasn't prepared. She's stunning. She reaches into her backpack and pulls out a container of sunscreen, smoothing it over her arms and legs, chest and belly. My eyes follow every movement, she's perfect.

"Can you put some of this on my back? I'm so jealous, you probably never burn." She smiles when I reach for it, turning and pulling her hair over her shoulder where she braids it quickly. I carefully smear sunscreen over her shoulders and upper back.

As I move towards her lower back, I notice she's holding *really* still. Goosebumps pop up all over the backs of her arms. *It's 90 degrees, I don't think she's cold.* Intrigued, I keep going, rubbing sunscreen carefully along her ribs to the edge of her bikini. I hear her let out a tiny sigh of pleasure, quickly squelched. *Down boy, this is not a good time to get excited.*

"All set," I announce, carefully snapping the cap shut. She turns and I hand her the tube of sunscreen. A blush is creeping up her cheeks.

"Thanks, do you need any?"

Not really, I sprayed some on at home.

"Yeah, it wouldn't hurt to put a little on my shoulders," I agree. "You're right, I don't burn easy, but it helps." I turn around and wait. It's worth the little white lie when her hands move across my back, firmly rubbing sunscreen across my shoulders, tickling lightly as she gets to my ribs. Hesitating only for a second, she smoothes the lotion across my lower back.

She's close enough that I can feel her breath flutter across my skin. I badly want to turn, gather her into my arms and continue the kiss we started in the market. Her fingers linger for a moment longer and then she draws away, closing the bottle.

"Do you want to go to the top of the falls? We can jump in from there and float through that gap and down the river a little ways," I point at each part of the route as I ask. Her eyes widen a tiny bit.

"Jump off the falls?" She looks up at the waterfall as if it's Niagara Falls not a fifteen foot bunny of a jump.

"Yeah, if you want to, the pool is pretty deep, no rocks. Come on, Girl, ready for a little adventure?" I'm teasing but I must have pushed a button somewhere because she stiffens and then squares her shoulders.

"Oh I am *jumping* off that waterfall, I am *so* doing that," Laurel mutters, marching past me and starting up the trail. She whispers something else about her age that I don't catch and then glances over her shoulder, smiling sheepishly.

"Sorry, you can lead, I just got excited," Laurel bites her lip, waiting for me to close the gap. I do, taking her hand and leading her up the trail and around the bend of the river that pours over the waterfall.

"It's shallow up here except in the very middle," I point, "we can walk up pretty close to the edge and it won't quite be knee deep. Just be careful, it can be a little slick." I lead the way out, walking carefully, until I'm standing a few feet from the edge, away from the faster current in the center. Laurel walks up beside me.

"This is beautiful, Trey, I've never been anywhere like this," she breathes, looking around in wonder. The birds are calling, flowers blooming along the banks of the river, clear blue water, it *is* pretty magical. We stand in silence for another moment until Laurel clears her throat lightly.

"Okay, before I lose my nerve, the pool is pretty deep right? I don't want to break my butt," she laughs nervously.

"Deep pool, no butt breaking," I confirm, smiling. "Jump out a little so the undertow of the falls doesn't spin you around, nothing to worry about. Want me to go first?"

"No, if you do, I'm afraid I won't jump at all," she laughs.

"Fair enough," I chuckle, backing up to give her some space and waving her ahead. Laurel scoots forward, leaning out to look over. I see her take a deep breath and wonder if she'll jump. Before I finish the thought Laurel takes a step and pushes off, launching herself out with a yell. She tucks her knees and lands in the water with a splash. When she surfaces a moment later, I see her head swivel around as she gets her bearings and then she swims smoothly to the large flat rock and climbs up to sit on the edge.

"That was awesome!" She yells up, a huge smile on her face, "Your turn!"

I back up and take a couple big steps forward, leaping off the cliff. Cutting through the water feet first, I surface and swim over to join Laurel on the rock. She's dangling her toes in the water, leaning back on her hands, smiling happily. Pushing up on the rock, I lean back on my elbows, enjoying the sun.

"We can hang here as long as you want and then I'll show you the next part." I lay back on the rock, hands behind my head.

"Thank you," Laurel whispers, looking down at me over her

shoulder.

"No thanks needed, I get to hang out with you," I reach over with one hand, lightly running my fingers down her back. Her eyes slide closed for a moment and then open, finding mine.

"No. I mean *thank you* for just expecting me to jump. You didn't assume I was scared, you didn't give me an out. I know that's not a huge waterfall," Laurel pauses, biting her lip, "but thank you for treating me like someone who takes a chance and just 'does the thing.'" She smiles, pulling her feet up on the rock and wrapping her arms around her knees. She rests her chin on her crossed arms, staring back at the waterfall.

"Well, you're welcome," she glances down at me and I grin at her, "I don't know what you're used to…but when I look at you, I see someone who's brave, and smart and beautiful. It just makes sense that you would, 'do the thing.'" I flex, so that I can use my hands to add air quotes and Laurel's eyes zoom in on my abs before trailing back up to my face. *Girl, you can eye bang me all you want, take the scenic route.* I put my hands back behind my head, waiting to see if she'll make a move.

Laurel doesn't disappoint. Leaning back on one elbow, she rolls up on her hip so she's stretched out beside me. Reaching over, her fingers follow the path her eyes just took. When they tickle along my collar bone, she leans down. Her braid has fallen out and strands of wet hair surround our faces like a curtain. She stares into my eyes for a second and then closes hers and kisses me.

Her hand slides up to hold my jaw and I let my head rest on the rock so that I can pull her close, feeling her body press up the length of mine. She's warm and soft, her lips demanding as she licks the seam of mine. Opening, I deepen the kiss, feeling her tongue swipe past mine. She rolls a little more so that she's fully straddling one of my thighs. I can feel her heat, *I wonder if she's wet for me.* The second the thought crosses my mind, I'm fully aroused, straining at my shorts.

Breaking the kiss with a groan, I let my head thunk softly on the rock, looking at Laurel. Her eyes are intent on me and we're both breathing harder. I was going to take a beat, get myself under control, but as I look in her eyes, I don't want to. Reaching up, I tangle my fingers in her hair, pulling her down to me, kissing her soundly.

Eventually, I'm forced to admit to myself that this rock is not the place for me to see if Laurel wants to take this further. It's a rock. Ending the kiss, I look at her, smiling.

"My kingdom for something soft under us right now," I joke and she laughs, sitting up carefully. I sit up with her, kissing her shoulder before I shift and slide off the rock into the water.

"Ready to do the next thing?" I hold on to the rock so that the light current of the river doesn't pull me away before she's ready to go. She smiles, scooting closer to the edge of the rock. The water is about shoulder deep on me, so I stand, reaching up and put my hands around her waist.

"This part we can do together," she hums a little 'oooooh' as I lift her into the water, her arms winding around my neck. I lift my feet and we're both floating with the current as I let it take us. We drift slowly across the length of the pool, the current steadily pulling us to a gap in the rocks.

"Trey, this is so cool," Laurel keeps hold of my shoulders, looking around as I lay back. The water is pleasantly cool after the heat of the rock.

"It gets a little faster up here, the rocks are smooth and the current will pull us down the middle though, it's fun." Laurel nods, her grip tightening a little, she turns to watch the rocks as we get closer. She lets out a happy little squeal as she feels the current take us, pulling us through the gap.

We float until the river widens and the current gets too slow to pull us. I stand, holding onto Laurel as we climb up the bank and walk back along the river's edge to the waterfall. As we let the sun dry us, Laurel gets out her camera, capturing some of the beauty of the falls. After a while she comes over and sits beside me, holding the camera out in front of us. She turns it to face us and scoots in close to me.

"Selfie time," she giggles, pushing the button. She takes a couple more and I turn my head, kissing her temple as I hear the shutter click. Leaning back a little, I look down at her as she looks up at me happily. I lean down and kiss her lips softly. *Kissing Laurel could easily become an addiction.*

"I think we're going to lose the light in about an hour, ready to head back?" I ask regretfully, I'm not ready to leave, but once the sun sets it is *dark* out here, no streetlights, only the moon to light our way. Laurel echoes my thoughts.

"I'm not really *ready*," Laurel smiles, "because this place is amazing…and I really like being with you." She ducks her head, suddenly shy, "but I bet it gets crazy dark with only moonlight through the trees out here." Standing, she brushes her legs off and puts her dress back on over her bikini. We both gather our things, zipping bags shut and walk hand in hand back to my motorcycle.

After a leisurely ride home, I pull up to her house and turn off the bike. Laurel gets off smoothly and I swing my leg over, standing beside the bike, leaning my butt on the seat. Reaching out, I take her hand and tug her in close. A smile curves her lips as she makes me work for it a little. I slide my arms around her waist.

"I've got some things to get done tomorrow that I can't put off, but will you have dinner with me tomorrow night?"

"Yes, I'd like that," she smiles up at me.

"I'll swing by around seven, we can ride to Margo's?" Laurel nods, her tongue flicking out to wet her lips, eyes on mine. *I see what you're doing there, girl.* Her eyes slide closed as I lean in, but fly back open when the breeze picks up, flipping a bunch of hair across her face, where it sticks to her lips. It breaks the moment when we both laugh, and I reach out, tucking the hair behind her ear and trailing my fingers along her jaw. Leaning in again, I kiss her.

It starts as a simple kiss, but her hands slide up my chest and into my hair. I wrap my arms around her waist, pulling her close. When we finally break the kiss to breathe, she lets go of my hair with a hum of pleasure and I force myself to loosen my arms and slide my hands to her hips. Kissing her softly one more time, I let go.

"See you tomorrow," I turn to go, but glance back at her, wanting a reason to stay. Her lips are plump and pink, strands of red hair floating around her face in the breeze. She gives me a sassy grin and reaches out, grabbing the front of my shirt and pulling. I let her pull me close and she stretches up on her toes, kissing me again, I feel her teeth graze my lip.

"Don't be late," she whispers. A blush steals up her cheeks as she lets go of me, turning and walking up the stairs to the deck of her house. She turns, smiling and gives me a little wave before she opens the door. I watch her until the door closes behind her, start my bike again and head for home.

The Hammock

L *aurel*

"So, tomorrow I'm going to the big island to meet some friends, kind of a last hurrah before we start circuit training...do you want to go with me?" Trey and I are sitting at his usual table on the edge of the deck, tucked into seared scallops on a seafood risotto that makes my stomach very, very happy.

"Sounds awesome, what's circuit training?" *I really hope that's not a stupid question.*

"My buddy Brian and I compete in the circuits every year, surfing," he explains, "um, we're pretty good, it's a lot of fun." He shrugs and keeps eating.

"Is there...any sort of dress code for tomorrow?" *That was an idiotic way to ask what I should wear.* Trey grins as if he can hear what I'm thinking.

"Nah, you look good in everything, it's casual, we'll just hit some bars, go dancing, whatever you want to do." There's heat in his eyes as he looks at me, it feels like a challenge. *Be brave, Laurel.*

"I'm up for anything," *don't blush, for the love of pete do not blush.* I force myself to look in his eyes. *This is the Age of Laurel. This time around, Laurel is brave.*

"I'm going to hold you to that, Girl," he finishes his food, tossing his napkin on the table. "You want to get out of here?"

Yes, especially if that is code for, let's go somewhere else so I can kiss you properly. I take my final drink of sangria and stand, waving at Margo across the bar. Trey smiles and ushers me off the deck, linking our fingers together as we walk along the moonlit beach.

"The night I saw you in the bar, Margo told me you left some drama back in the city…" Trey hesitates, I feel my eyebrows try to meet in the middle as I react with a frown. "If you don't want to talk about it, that's cool," he continues, stopping and pulling me into a hug, "but I'm all ears if you need them."

"It all feels kind of far away now," I shrug, looking up into his eyes. "I mean, I guess *technically* it is geographically quite far away now as well." I pause, waiting for the painful little zing to lay my heart open again. Nothing.

"Whatever happened, it must have been kind of rough to make you come all the way to this tiny island," Trey says softly. With his arms circling my waist, his hands conveniently rest on the upper swell of my butt. *I like it a lot.*

"Well, long story short, I was dating a guy. I thought things were great, I brought him coffee one morning and found out that another woman had spent the night in his bed." The words tumble out as if it won't hurt if I say it fast. "The *real* kick in the teeth was that the other woman was my best friend. I've known her since primary school,"

"Ouch," Trey murmurs slowly.

"Yeah, *that* was a big ouch." I laugh softly. "Anyhoo…I bailed and I'm here, which has worked out pretty well so far…" An embarrassing little squeal escapes me when Trey's arms tighten and he lifts me up in the air, his lips crashing down on mine. I wrap my arms around his neck and kiss him back.

"Pretty well is an understatement," Trey whispers when I'm finally forced to pull away for a breath. He gently sets my feet back in the sand and takes my hand. Linking our fingers he brings them up to his lips, grazing a kiss across my knuckles as we start walking along the shore again.

I recognize the cluster of trees that juts close to the ocean just before his house comes into view. Stopping near a tree with a large bend in one of its low branches, he leans into it like a seat, pulling me close. There's just enough moonlight that his eyes find mine, and he leans in, kissing me softly. Reaching up, I tangle my fingers in his hair, pulling him closer, and kiss him hard, parting my lips. He tightens his arms around me with a groan, his tongue flicking against mine. His hands slide down my back, skim over my ass, and he grabs my thighs, lifting me up. I let my legs wrap around his waist, our lips still welded together, and nothing has ever felt so right in my life.

When we break the kiss to breathe, his lips trail along my jaw and he nips the side of my neck. I know I have to be getting heavy, clinging to him like a monkey, but his hands easily hold my ass as he sits in the bend of the tree. My eyes want to flutter shut when he nips my collarbone. Just before they do, I see a large hammock swaying in the breeze between two other trees nearby.

Unwrapping my legs from his hips, I slide down his body

until my feet hit the sand, giving a little shiver as I notice he's packing some heat. Leaning up to kiss him again, I pull him toward the hammock. As I get closer, I start to question the logistics of hammock cuddling. That is, until Trey gathers my hair in his fist, moving it out of the way and kissing the side of my neck, letting me feel a hint of his teeth. *We'll figure it out, ohmygod that's good.*

Kissing me again, hard, Trey lets me go and moves to the hammock, sitting in the center and smoothly flipping his legs in so he's laying in the middle. His eyes are full of heat as he looks at me. He flexes, reaching over his shoulders and pulling his shirt off in one motion. *Ping-ping-ping.* Standing close to the edge of the hammock, I run a finger along his ribs, hoping I look sultry. Flipping my hair out of my face, I climb in the hammock like a panther stalking prey.

Well...the *idea* was sultry, awesome, sexy panther stuff...the result is...not. *Clearly physics, geometry, or whatever explains how hammocks work, is not in my wheelhouse.* I put my knee on the edge of the hammock, planning to do a sexy crawl that lands me next to Trey. In theory, *hot*, in practice, a huge mistake. Trey's eyes widened the moment I put my weight into my knee to climb on. Of course, once I put my weight on my knee, I'm committed.

I let out a shriek as the hammock tips, my body sprawling across Trey's waist. The far edge of the hammock hits me directly in the face before flipping us to the sand below. I land flat on my back, gasping like a fish. Trey manages to catch himself, landing in kind of a push-up over my middle.

"That went...so much better...in my head," I gasp. Trey bursts out laughing, turning on his hands and stretching out in the sand at my side. He smoothes the hair back from my face, his

54

touch soft. His hand hovers for a second and his brows draw together as he looks closer at my face. He touches my lips with one fingertip. It feels weird.

"I think you're…sandy," Trey laughs and I touch my own lips. He's right. A lot of sand hit us both when I flipped the hammock, my lipgloss is now completely coated. *Note to self, if I survive this night, no more lip gloss.* First the wind earlier and now sand, *cripes*.

As I try to figure out a way to gracefully wipe my lips, *it's probably going to involve some very unsexy spitting, eww,* I see movement behind Trey's shoulder. Hidden in the shadows by Trey's deck, something is moving. It takes a few steps towards us and I freeze when I see black and white fur.

"Ohmygod, Trey, there's a skunk behind you!" I panic-whisper, accidentally eating a few grains of lip gloss flavored sand in the process. He startles, flexing, well, *everything* as he looks over his shoulder.

A second later, he collapses back in the sand, laughing. The animal walks a little closer…*it's clearly a cat*, headbutting Trey and rubbing all over his shoulder. Trey sits up, scooping up the cat and scratching between her ears. A loud purr thrums out of the cat as her eyes close with delight.

"Laurel, meet Ollie," Trey has a great laugh. It's infectious and I can't help but join him, mostly out of relief.

"Hi, Ollie," I gasp, still laughing, "thank you for not being a skunk." Trey gets to his feet, letting the cat down. She winds around his ankles, staring at me. He holds out his hands and when I take them, pulls me up to stand with him.

"Do you want to come in?" Trey's eyes are intense, his hands resting on my hips. *Oh man, I really, really, really do…but, if this is any indication of how tonight is going to go, I think my mojo is broken.*

"Regretfully, I think I'm going to go home and de-sand myself," reaching up, I brush a finger across his lips. "Second order of business is to throw away all my lipgloss." Trey chuckles, letting go of my hips. Leaning forward, he kisses my cheek and I feel his breath flutter across my ear.

"Until tomorrow then," he whispers. *Ping-ping-ping.*

The Secret Ingredient

T rey

I'm up early, getting things together at the house before I go to the marina to check the boat. I've got a 36-footer with a cabin below the deck. It used to belong to my parents, but my dad's knees ended their sailing days a while back.

Everything set, I head for Margo's. It's early enough that business is slow, I see Laurel and Margo behind the bar, a number of bottles and containers of fruit lined up in front of them. They haven't seen me yet, so I just lean on a tree in the shade off the deck and watch quietly.

"Now, Chica," Margo's face is serious but she's clearly trying not to smile, "here's the 'secret' part of this recipe…don't laugh and *don't tell anyone.*" She turns and opens a small cupboard at the end of the counter. With a broad smile she presents Laurel a little packet no bigger than the palm of her hand. Laurel stares at it a moment and bursts into giggles.

"The secret ingredient of your sangria is a packet of cherr-" the rest of her words are muffled as Margo covers her mouth quickly, laughing and looking around dramatically as if Laurel is revealing dangerous intel.

"It's a *secret* Chica! Oh, hey Trey, didn't see you arrive, you want to taste test Laurel's first batch?" Margo transitions smoothly, dropping her hand away from Laurel, who is still laughing.

"Sounds good," I take a seat across from them as Margo busies herself capping several bottles. Laurel pulls three glasses from the shelf and pours for all of us, sliding mine to me with a smile.

"Good morning," she whispers, "I'm glad you still showed up after my epic sequence of disasters last night."

"Oh I wouldn't call *any* of that a *disaster*," I counter, teasing. "Although you may need to formally apologize to Ollie for calling her a skunk." Reaching over, I tap the rim of my glass against hers, taking a drink. She takes a drink of her own, blushing. Margo comes back to the counter, picking up her own glass and takes a drink. She makes a big show of swishing it around in her mouth and swirling the glass.

"Excellent vintage, Chica," she laughs, "and now, you guys are probably ready to get going huh? Big island day?"

"Big island day," Laurel agrees, quickly wiping the counter and throwing the cloth in the sink. I toss back the rest of my sangria and stand.

"Big island day," I echo, smiling at Laurel and holding out my arm. She affects a regal air and takes my elbow with a grin.

* * *

"I could do this forever," Laurel raises her voice to be heard over the noise of the engine. She's sitting at the front of the boat, legs curled under her, hair streaming down her back, face to the wind. I don't bother to respond, she wouldn't hear me anyway. The boat ride to Brian's *usually* takes a little less than an hour. Laurel loves the boat ride so much, I've slowed it down and we're coming around the island by a longer route.

Once we get close to the shore, I slow the boat even more, giving Laurel a chance to look at the fancy places along the beach. We're meeting Brian and his girlfriend at a bar situated on a small bay. I coast us up and dock the boat, offering Laurel a hand up.

"This is beautiful Trey," she breathes, stumbling slightly when the boat rocks on a swell right as she steps to the dock. Steadying her with an arm around her waist, I give her a squeeze.

"It's all right, I guess. I'd rather look at you." Laurel smiles at my words, ducking her head to hide a blush. She's wearing the flower, clipped in her hair just behind her ear. Her shirt is short sleeved, cropped so I can see a tease of golden skin peeking above the waist of her jeans. The legs of her jeans are so wide it looks like she's wearing a skirt. The material must be lighter than real denim, because it flutters in the breeze.

"Duuuuuude! You made it!" Brian's familiar call reaches us before he does. He comes jogging down the dock, yanking me into a one armed hug.

"And hello, Pretty!" He turns to Laurel, hugging her too. She's caught up in his infectious energy, giggling as he sets her back on her feet. Everything is always full throttle with Brian.

"Brian, this is Laurel," we follow him up the dock towards the bar. I can hear other voices and music.

"Dude, I *know*, we *clearly* just met," Brian laughs, turning back to wink at Laurel.

"Right, right, *jackass*," I mutter the last part under my breath, knowing Brian will hear me. He looks back and laughs again.

"I've missed you, man, Meg's holding a table for us, let's grab drinks!" Brian leads the way. The bar is crowded, the music is loud, and Laurel's skin is warm under my hand.

Was That an Earthquake?

L *aurel*

Everyone seems to be talking and laughing and having fun, Trey keeps an arm around my waist, leaning in to whisper-yell introductions as he sees friends along the way. Brian pushes his way up to the bar, yells an order and starts handing us drinks.

As we wind through the crowd, Trey steers me to the table guarded by Meg, who turns out to be a tall, leggy blonde with a million-watt smile.

"Trey, lookin' good kid!" Meg raises her drink in a toast, clearly a few ahead of us. "And who's this pretty?"

"Meg, this is Laurel," Trey leans in to give her a quick hug and then she turns to give me a full appraisal.

"Laurel, it's a pleasure. Good luck taming this guy," she hiccups, tossing back the rest of her drink and looking around expectantly. "Where's Brian? I'm emp-tyyyy."

"Relax my love, drinks are here," Brian laughs, setting a round on the table. He's brought me something fruity, complete with an umbrella. Taking a quick sip I taste a lot of rum, it's delicious. Brian and Trey start talking about the upcoming weeks of training, it sounds like a lot of early mornings, but I don't catch many other details.

"So what's your story, Laurel?" Meg scoots closer, scrutinizing me carefully. *Well shit, friend's protective girlfriend alert...*

"Oh, there's not much to tell," I start carefully, "I've been on the island for about a week."

"Yeah, yeah, that's boring," Meg laughs, "I want to hear how *you* managed to snag Trey Blake, the island's most *reclusive* bachelor." She wiggles her eyebrows mysteriously, the last few words echoed by her glass as she takes another drink. *Well gee, Meg, I'll start by trying not to take offense at the little emphasis you put on 'you'.*

"My dad and his wife run a bar on the island. Trey likes to have dinner there, we met when I arrived about a week ago," I shrug, glancing at Trey to see if he's listening. His blue eyes meet mine and he grins. *That* grin, *ping-ping.* I think he was paying attention, curious about what I would say to Meg, so I turn the tables.

"Reclusive, huh? Do tell."

Meg leans forward, delighted, when Trey slides an arm around my waist, abruptly standing up from the table. He *literally* lifts me up with him, *I feel a mini earthquake hit my clit, that caveman thing completely flips my switch.*

"Dance with me," he rumbles in my ear, tucking me close to his side. Meg laughs and waves us off, turning to talk to Brian. Trey leads me to the center of the dance floor. Turning, he pulls me towards him, spinning me into his chest. He smiles as

I laugh helplessly, just along for the ride. Holding me close, we settle into the beat, moving together.

"I wouldn't say *reclusive,*" Trey leans downs close to my ear as he speaks. "It just makes Meg crazy that I live on the quiet island and turn down all of her attempts to set me up with her friends."

"I sort of think that *defines* reclusive," I laugh, looking up to make sure he can tell I'm teasing.

"Fair point," he shrugs, leaning down and nuzzling the side of my neck in a way that sends shivers *everywhere,* "maybe I was just waiting for you." *Ohgoodlord I'm dizzy.*

Tequila and a Keeper

T rey

Meg and Brian hit the dance floor soon after we do, handing us new drinks and then laughing and grinding like high school kids. We dance for a long time, until I realize the bar is so packed that it's hard to move and it's getting hot. I lean down so she can hear me.

"Want to get some air?"

Laurel nods, linking her fingers with mine. I get Brian's attention and then head for the waterfront side of the bar. Once we get away from the dance floor, I can feel a light breeze. There's a big row of lounge chairs and I head for the end, sinking into one with a sigh and tugging Laurel into my lap. Brian flops into the chair next to us.

"Where's Meg?" Laurel asks him, leaning back into me with a sigh.

"Lil' girls room, then drinks, I think," Brian stretches out in the chair, closing his eyes. He looks like he's going to fall asleep, but he keeps talking.

"So what's your deal anyway, you two?" Brian is slurring ever so slightly, and he cracks an eye to look at us. Laurel shifts, glancing over her shoulder at me as he rambles on. "Meg told me to ask…she said to be subtle but…well clearly that's not happening."

"Does there need to be a 'deal'?" I ask lightly. "We met a week ago, dude." I trail my fingers up and down Laurel's arm, she relaxes again.

"Got it, got it, you know Meg, always lookin' for a fucking label." Brian holds up his hands in surrender. "She's just annoyed that you found someone without her help," he laughs and I can't help but laugh with him, thinking about all of the dates I dodged and the few disasters I didn't manage to escape.

"Are you guys laughing about my matchmaking skills?" Meg manages to pass the drinks out without a drop lost, handing hers to Brian as she settles herself in front of him, leaning against his stomach. Reaching for her drink, she gives him a little elbow in the gut. "Sounds like you were super subtle, Lover, nice job."

"Eh, you know you love me anyway," Brian scoffs.

In the silence that follows, Brian's words start knocking around in my head. *Is there a 'deal'? Maybe there should be…* I know I don't want Laurel to go anywhere, I know I want to see where this goes. That'll have to be enough. *Yeah…there's a deal.*

* * *

65

"I'm bored, next bar!" Meg announces, jiggling the ice around in her glass. Standing up she pulls Brian to his feet and then looks at me questioningly.

"You guys ready?" Brian's got his second wind, bouncing on the balls of his feet, he leans in and bites Meg's shoulder lightly. She squeals, slapping at his arm.

Laurel sits up and looks at me, eyes sparkling. *Well, she did say she's up for 'whatever'.*

"Let's do it," I agree. Putting my hands on Laurel's hips, I lift her to standing and then get up myself, wrapping my arms around her from behind.

"Let's do it!" Brian echoes, swatting Meg on the ass, he jogs ahead of her, leading the way up the boardwalk, laughing when she flips him off.

* * *

The night is full of music, drinks and laughing. Meg and Brian tell Laurel *way* too many stories about stupid shit I've done. Meg pries until Laurel tells her a little bit about her work and her life before she came to the island, she doesn't mention her breakup. *I hope it's because she's so into me she can't even remember that fucker.*

Laughing at the most recent 'listen to this stupid-ass thing Trey did one time' story, Laurel pushes away from the table, giving me a wink as she heads for the bar.

"Oooo-girl got a *plan*, looks like," Meg giggles. She and Brian start another one of their drunk little kiss-pinch things while I watch Laurel. Her skin glows golden in the lights, hair cascading down her back, flicking against the skin visible at her waist. She flips it back over her shoulder as she leans up on tiptoe to talk to the bartender. He nods and starts pouring. While she waits, she looks back over her shoulder at me.

I want her. I want her bad. She might be a mind-reader, because I swear she stares right across the bar at me, licks her lips and smiles. *I see what you're doing there, Girl.*

A minute later, Laurel's walking across the bar, eyes on the tray she's trying to balance. She sets it down triumphantly and I swear it sounds an awful lot like she's humming a song.

"Tequila shots! I knew we were gonna be besties!" Meg squeals her approval.

"Oh I'm going to pay for these, but they are *happening*! Neck or belly-button?" Brian grabs the salt, eyes on Meg who giggles and points at her cleavage. I eye the tray of shots, lime wedges and salt, then look at Laurel. She blushes, but her chin raises defiantly.

"You up for this, Trey?" she asks teasingly, before leaning closer, her next words for me alone. "I've never actually done this before, but we've got to make our 'big island day' memorable, right?" *Perfect. She is fucking perfect.* I lean in close, letting my lips touch her ear.

"I'm ready for anything that gives me an excuse to lick you," I lean back just in time to see her eyes slide closed for a second. When she opens them, she gives me a smile full of heat and naughty promises, then hands me the salt. Gently pushing her hair back off her shoulder, I hook a finger in the waistband of her pants, pulling her closer.

Leaning in, I lick her shoulder, kissing it before I sprinkle on a little salt. She tilts her head, breath coming a little faster, watching me. I put my mouth to her shoulder again, but instead of simply licking the salt, I suck on her skin for just a moment, enjoying her little gasp. Downing the shot, I savor the burn and reach for a lime.

"My turn," Laurel whispers, oblivious to Meg giggling and Brian busily trying to salt her boobs.

Laurel gives me a nudge, pushing me towards a chair. "You're too tall," she laughs softly, stepping up between my knees. I don't know what to do with my hands, so I settle them on her hips. *I am so fucking hot for her right now that I'm mostly just thinking about anything that will keep every drop of blood in my body from abandoning my brain.*

I can smell her perfume as she leans in, her finger slides my collar out of the way and I feel her lips, soft on my collar bone right before she licks me. Our eyes meet as she reaches for the salt, *she knows what she's doing to me right now.* I feel a few grains hit my neck. As she leans in to lick them off, I reach for the lime. *Two can play that game.* Laurel downs her shot and looks at me again, smiling through the burn as she sees me holding the lime in my mouth. Her lips crash into mine and she sucks on the lime, one hand sliding up my shoulder to hold the back of my neck.

"Brian, get a pitcher of water quick, I think those two are gonna burst into flames!" Meg heckles, dropping her own lime in an empty glass. Laurel lets go of me, the lime between her lips. She follows Meg's example, tossing it in an empty glass and smiles brightly.

"What's next?"

Brian laughs, throwing an arm around Laurel's shoulders.

"Oh, I like this one Trey, this one's a keeper. C'mon, let's go do a bonfire."

A Bonfire Before Bed

*L*aurel

Brian lives in a huge bungalow, most of it open to the beach, just down the boardwalk from downtown. Curling up in a lounge chair with Trey, I stare at the stars and enjoy the fire. This night is perfect. Meg and Brian are in the house mixing martinis, *they must have livers of absolute steel.* Trey brought me a big glass of juice.

"If I'm going to get you to make a bad decision, I want to know you're sober," he said solemnly, before cracking a grin that almost blew my clothes off.

The night air is cool, but Trey is warm, arms wrapped around me, I feel his breath in my hair. It's pleasant, watching the fire. Trey's fingers start tickling a slow path up and down my arm, *it feels like the best kind of anticipation.*

We've watched the fire burn, it's mostly just coals, when I realize that Meg and Brian haven't come outside. I'm about to say something, when I hear Meg giggle. Glancing up, I can see that the balcony doors are wide open, Brian is carrying her, they are silhouetted by the light in the room for just a moment before he appears to toss her on the bed. They're both laughing and then one of them turns off the light. *Well...that's awkward.*

Trey and I are both silent, but I think we realize at the same time that Meg and Brian are probably going to get a whole lot louder. Our movements are almost synchronized as we sit up and look at each other. Trey reaches for me, pulling me up with him and we walk to the boat.

"Did you have some juice or something too? You cool to drive us back?" I hate to be a wet blanket, but it seems fair to ask. Trey smiles.

"I was thinking maybe we could sleep on the boat tonight, go back in the morning? The water is calm and the stars are bright." His voice is low, full of promise.

Yeah, that'll give me plenty of time to make one of those decisions he mentioned earlier. Oh boy, I don't think it'll be a bad one.

"*That* is a much better plan," I smile, taking his hand as I step on the boat.

Trey leads me below the deck, there's a very short hallway with a tiny bathroom on one side and some sort of storage on the other. The hallway opens into a bedroom. Trey pauses at the doorway, glancing over his shoulder at me. I walk up close behind him, sliding my hands around his waist and rest my cheek on his back.

He sighs, leaning his head back on the top of mine as I let my hands roam under his shirt, feeling the hard planes of his stomach, trailing along the edge of his shorts. He captures one of my hands, turning around slowly. He kisses my hand and sits on the edge of the bed, tugging me to stand between his knees.

"I didn't mean we *can't* go back tonight," Trey says slowly. He looks up, his eyes searching my face. "We're only staying here if you want to…and I'm not expecting anything." *Ohhhh he is officially perfect.* Sliding my hands up his shoulders, I hold his jaw, running my thumb over his lower lip as I just breathe for a second.

"There is not one fiber of my being that doesn't want to stay here, with you, tonight…" It's the truth, I want him. *I stun myself with my own bravery as I continue,* "and I think I *am* expecting… something." Trey's lips stretch in a smile, his eyes filling with heat. His hand slides up my back into my hair and he pulls me down, our lips meeting as he *kisses* me.

His lips move against mine and I open, feeling the flick of his tongue. It feels like he's tasting me, it's sensual and naughty and I *really* want more. Deepening the kiss, I let my hands wander under his shirt, finally just pushing it up over his chest. He breaks the kiss long enough to pull it quickly over his head and then his lips find mine again.

Trey's hands grip my hips and then move to the button of my pants, popping it open and sliding them off my hips, his lips moving along my collarbone. I bring my knees up on the bed, straddling him and pushing him on his back. I can feel him, hard against his jeans and he gives a low groan as I rock my hips over him slowly.

I lean down to kiss him again and he wraps his arms tight around my back, rolling us so that my back is on the bed. Everywhere his breath touches my skin feels like a lick of flame as he pushes up my shirt. The bralette I'm wearing isn't much more than an obligatory triangle of lace, his thumb scrapes it aside and my eyes roll back as I feel his tongue.

71

Kissing his way down my belly, he pauses long enough that I come out of my haze and look down at him.

"I like these," he tugs on the lace of my thong with his teeth and then, still looking at me, pushes them to the side. As he lets me feel the heat of his breath, my eyes slide shut and he shoulders my legs far apart. *My vagina just went Defcon 1.*

If the Boat's Rocking...

T *rey*

My dick is straining against my jeans and it's all I can do not to grind against the bed. Laurel's hips are rocking slowly, I can tell she's close. Popping the button on my jeans to relieve some pressure, I shove them off my hips. I stop teasing her and focus on her clit, I feel her fingers in my hair as she falls over the edge with a choked cry.

Standing, I put my hands under her hips and pull her to the edge of the bed. Reaching for my bag, I grab a condom and tear it open. Laurel watches me, licking her lips and running a hand up my chest. She digs her nails in and my hips jerk. I lean down to kiss her hard, she wraps her legs around my waist and moans as I thrust deep.

"Oh, fuckkk Trey, yes!" Laurel's whisper turns into a throaty yell as I pick her up, still buried deep. Turning, I brace her back against the wall and start pounding, hard and fast. Her arms are around my shoulders, fingers tangled in my hair, I hold her thighs tight.

"Come for me again, Girl," I grit out. Laurel gasps and I feel her lips on my neck right before she sets her teeth in my shoulder. That tiny bit of pain pushes me over the edge. I feel her clenching around me as I find my release and she lets her head fall back against the wall with a soft moan.

There's no sound but our breathing for a few moments. I crack a grin and Laurel giggles as we realize at the same time that the boat is rocking gently. I turn, setting her on the bed and stretching out beside her as I pull her in close. I like it when she immediately reaches for me again, her fingers playing across my ribs. Reaching down, I pull one of the sheets up over us and kiss her shoulder. She gives a little hum of contentment and we sleep.

* * *

When I wake up, the sun is streaming in through one of the tiny portholes and Laurel is gone. Pulling on some shorts, I walk up the stairs to the deck and she's stretched out on her stomach in the sun, reading. She looks over her shoulder and smiles at me, giving her butt a little wiggle that makes me want to drag her right back down the stairs.

"Morning, Sleepy. I would have made you breakfast, but I didn't find a kitchen hidden in any of the closets," she teases, marking her book. She tosses it aside and sits up.

"Oh no, breakfast is *my* department," my stomach is already groaning in anticipation. "I'm taking you to The Diner."

"In that case, let me jump in the shower quick," Laurel stands, walking over and putting a hand on my chest as she leans up and kisses me.

"Sure…it's big enough for two," she gives a little squeal and wraps her arms around my neck as I scoop her up and take her back downstairs. I take her to bed first, *to make sure we've got an appetite, of course. The meals at The Diner are huge. Also, I want to hear her sigh my name again…and again.*

Let's Go Sailing

~~~ §◦§ ~~~

L *aurel*

Strolling the boardwalk with Trey, the sun warm on our backs, I am completely happy. I can smell The Diner before I see it and I start picturing a pile of buttermilk pancakes and lots of bacon. When we round the corner, it is as cute as the name implies.

The Diner is one of those long silver restaurants with a counter running the full length of the wall, waitresses in little pink dresses with aprons and sensible shoes. The whole place has a very 'throwback to the 50's' vibe, right down to the jukebox in the corner.

Several of the people sitting along the counter and in the booths seem to know Trey as we walk in, he responds with smiles and little waves, ushering me to an open booth in the center of the row.

"Mornin' folks, somethin' to drink?" The waitress is a smiling woman in her forties with light brown hair.

"Mmm, yes please, orange juice and coffee." I can smell the bacon and my stomach is going nuts.

"Same for me, thanks Judy," Trey smiles at her and then flips open the menu. "I don't know why I look at this, I always get the same exact thing, they just call it 'The Big Plate'," he laughs.

Judy takes our order, dropping off the juice and coffee. Trey takes a sip of coffee, sitting back in the booth with a sigh.

"I don't want to take you home yet," his eyes are bright, a smile hovering at the corner of his mouth, "what would you say to a few days on the boat? Just you, me, the sun and the water? I could show you some more of the islands."

"I'd say, I'll need a quick stop at the house for some clothes and a big bottle of sunscreen," I smile back, my stomach fluttering with delight, "but if you're serious, that sounds amazing."

"Oh, I'm serious." Trey glances up as our food arrives. Judy checks our mugs, grabbing the coffee pot off the counter and refilling them with practiced ease before moving on to the next table.

"Will a side trip get in the way of training?" I ask, as we dig into our food. The bacon is crispy and the pancakes are golden, I pour syrup over the whole works and look up at Trey.

"Nah, I'll bring a board in case we dock anywhere with good waves, Brian is more gung-ho than I am," Trey shrugs, eyes on his food.

"I need to grab my camera too," I muse, "and maybe my laptop."

"Sure thing, we can stay out as long as we want to, there's good beaches and restaurants everywhere. Hell, the first major competition I'm looking at is still two months away," he smiles,

"I might never bring you back."

"Do you think...could you show me some surfing stuff? Nothing fancy, just maybe how to not fall off?" *Why am I blushing?*

"Absolutely," Trey actually looks excited at the prospect, "we could tandem too, I think you'd like that, I'll pack some extra gear."

A trip...really? You haven't known him very long...what are you doing? A small part of my brain starts piping in from the cheap seats. As we keep eating, I think about it...and decide I don't care. This brave, new Laurel is going to go for what she wants, and I want Trey.

I'm about half-way through my ridiculously large pile of pancakes and bacon when Trey's plate is empty. I push mine in his direction and he digs in, laughing. I sit back and watch him, drinking my coffee, full and happy and ready for an adventure.

Wow, She's Brave

T rey

Walking back to the boat, we talk about what we'll need to be out for a few days and places Laurel might like to see. We sail home at a leisurely pace, arriving early afternoon.

"How about dinner at Margo's tonight and we sail out tomorrow morning?" I gather her in my arms before she goes inside.

"Mhmmm, that sounds perfect," she tilts her face up and closes her eyes as I kiss her, long and slow. After a moment I let her go, even though I don't want to, "See you later, then." She smiles and goes into the house.

I call Bonnie on the way home. She's in high school, likes to make extra money when I'm travelling by taking care of Ollie. Shooting my agent and Brian quick texts, I figure that's enough responsibility for today and start getting my gear ready.

Loading my jeep, I head for the marina a couple hours later, getting the boat squared away so there's not much to do but sail out tomorrow.

When I arrive at Margo's, Laurel is having a drink with her dad. She smiles when she sees me.

"Trey, hey, join us?" Laurel motions me over to the table. "You've met my dad, Williams?"

"Never officially," Williams stands, offering his hand. I shake it and we both take our seats as Margo brings me a beer, patting my shoulder as she heads back for food.

"I understand you're taking my daughter sailing for a few days," Williams has a deep, cultured voice. I realize that it's funny that in all the nights I've eaten here, we've never had a conversation.

"That's right, I thought I'd show her some of the other islands in the group, there's a lot to photograph. She also wants to learn to surf." I toss Laurel a little wink, she laughs.

"Well, to clarify, I want to learn some very basic stuff like not drowning and not falling down constantly," she adds, "I've seen Trey surfing and that is just, wow."

"You'll certainly have a good teacher," Williams agrees. "It is not an everyday occurrence that one has the opportunity to learn from a world champion, after all." He takes a small drink of his whiskey and I see Laurel's eyes widen.

"World champion?" She blushes, "Oh wow...I didn't know, you don't have to teach me, Trey."

"Why wouldn't I?" I tease, wondering what the big deal is, *it's certainly not me.*

"Well, duh, I mean *World Champion?* I'm just feeling like an asshole that I didn't know," she reaches over and smacks Williams in the shoulder, "why didn't you tell me before?" He looks surprised.

"I believe this is one of those instances where it did not occur to me that the information would be of immediate importance," Williams responds, glancing from Laurel to me. "At some point I can only assume it would have come up in conversation, which it has at just this moment." He looks out at the bar over my shoulder, his eyes narrowing.

I look back to see what has caught Williams' attention and see a woman entering the bar, looking around uncertainly. She's a tall black woman, her skin glowing in the light. She flips dark curls back off her shoulder, looking around before noticing us, clearly recognizing Williams and Laurel.

"What the fresh hell are you doing here?" Margo's voice cuts across the music and several nearby conversations screech to a halt. Laurel looks up, confused, turning to see what's going on. She gasps when she sees the woman, who is clearly uncomfortable under Margo's gaze.

"Gabs?" Laurel's voice is uncertain. Her next words are firmer as she gets over her surprise. Standing, she takes a few steps towards the newcomer, folding her arms across her chest. "Why would you come here?"

Suddenly it clicks who this woman is and why her welcome is on the arctic side of frosty. *This is the best friend that slept with her ex.* Standing, I walk up behind Laurel, putting my hands on her shoulders. She reaches up and covers one of my hands with her own.

"We can't leave things the way we did, Laurel," Gabrielle puts out her hands, trying to placate Laurel, "we need to talk."

"We don't have anything to talk about, Gabs. You've wasted a trip," Laurel scowls, huffing out a sigh.

"I don't believe that, Laurel," Gabs insists defiantly. "I would

81

have been here sooner but I didn't know where you'd gone and you wouldn't answer my calls. I had to wait and figure it out when you posted on your blog again." She walks closer, a pleading look in her eyes as she stares at Laurel. "Can we talk, please?"

Laurel doesn't answer for a long moment, but based on the little bit of the story I've heard, Gabs has been her friend for a long time. Leaning forward, I whisper in her ear.

"Go ahead and take my table."

"Let's talk then," Laurel sighs, giving my hand a squeeze, she walks over to my usual table and sits down. Gabs follows her, sitting across from her carefully. Other conversations have started to resume, Margo is still watching them, but has started pouring drinks again, shoulders stiff with anger.

Walking over to the bar, I get Margo's attention.

"How about I take them a couple glasses of sangria?" Margo focuses on me, nodding as she visibly tries to relax.

"Good idea, thanks, Trey." She looks at Laurel and Gabs again, "do you know who that is?"

"Yes and I know why you're so angry…I also know they've been friends for a long time."

"The best," Margo is still heated, "how *she* could let a man come between them…" she trails off, pouring two glasses of sangria and setting them in front of me before grabbing a cloth and fiercely cleaning the counter.

See? Rhombus.

L aurel

Trey walks towards our table, two glasses of sangria in his hands. I stand and meet him halfway.

"Thanks, but you should have brought just one, she doesn't deserve this deliciousness," I scowl. Trey grins.

"Watch them claws, Girl," leaning down, he kisses my nose, "do you want me to stay here a while, wait for you?"

"Oh, no, that's okay, I guess I better hear her out," I huff out a sigh, "can I come find you later?"

"I'll be at my house, it doesn't matter how late, come on over," he hesitates, "we can still leave tomorrow if you still want to go." *I want to curl up in his arms and forget everything else.*

"I still want to go," I nod my head firmly and he smiles.

"I'll see you later then," he squeezes my hand and steps off the deck, heading for home. I turn back to Gabs, setting one of the sangria in front of her with a sigh.

"I'm only giving you that because it would be weird to sit here and drink them both in front of you," I announce.

"Understood," Gabs lets a tiny smile stretch her lips and leans forward, taking a drink. "Ohmygod that's good."

"Yeah, I know." I grunt, still not sure if I want to hear what she has to say. We lapse into an uncomfortable silence. Gabs opens and closes her mouth several times, taking a deep breath as if she's going to talk, but keeps losing her nerve. Finally, I decide to throw my cards on the table first because I don't want to waste any more time and I'm not interested in excuses.

"If you wanted Mace, I would have backed off," I fiddle with the rim of my glass, my feelings pinballing between angry and sad. "What hurts the most is that you would throw away all the years we've been friends for a man I dated for a few months. *A few months!*" I look up at her and see her eyes brimming with tears. "Was it because he was famous?" She chokes out a little sob and the tears start to rain down her cheeks. *You're not getting out of this with tears, not today Gabs.*

"If you're just gonna cry, I'm gonna need more sangria," I snarl, tipping over into just angry. I stand and walk to the bar. Margo watches me approach and then reaches down and grabs a pitcher. Filling it, she hands it to me without a word. *Now we're talking.*

Stomping back to our table, I fill both our glasses.

"Let's go to the beach," I say abruptly, grabbing the pitcher and leaving my glass behind as I step off the deck into the sand. Gabs picks up her own glass and follows. We walk out into the quiet moonlight, wandering without speaking until we reach my rock. Stopping, I climb up and scoot over, waiting for her to join me.

We sit on the rock, drinking and watching the waves and

not speaking for a long time. Finally, I hear Gabs take a deep breath.

"It had nothing to do with him being famous," Gabs says bitterly.

"Then why Gabs? Drunk, sad, stupid, lonely? Just wanted a fuck? What the hell was he offering you that made it worth throwing away *years* of being best friends?" Using both hands, I tip up the pitcher, taking a big drink. *This is no way to handle my feelings. Well...this is an unhealthy way to handle my feelings. Whatever.*

"None of those things…" Gabs says slowly, taking another drink. "I didn't even want him, really."

"What the fuck, Gabs." I'm in disbelief.

"Yeah, what the fuck. I *know*, Laurel," she turns, glaring right at me, "you don't understand." Gabs climbs back off the rock, walking away into the sand. Grumbling, *because I'm confused now and also I have to carry this damn pitcher every time we go sit somewhere different,* I follow.

"Pretty fucking difficult to understand why you would throw *us* away if you won't tell me." I say to her back as I watch the breeze whip her hair.

She turns, mutely holding out her glass. I pour, noticing that the pitcher is about killed and my balance is not holding up. Sitting down in the sand, I park the pitcher before I spill those last precious ounces of sangria and decide to wait her out.

"It's hard to understand because you've never seen *us* like I do," Gabs finally speaks, still turned away.

"What does *that* mean," *I'm tipsy is probably what that means, I'm probably missing something big here.* "We've been best friends since primary school, we've done every important thing in our lives together since. How do I not see us?" I sigh, laying back

85

on the sand, done with the whole thing.

Gabs sits beside me in the sand, staring out at the ocean.

"You see us as best friends, that's true, we've been that for a long time," Gabs whispers. "I slept with Mace because I was angry and drunk and it made sense at the time."

"Angry? I hadn't seen you in weeks, what the fuck were you angry about?" I'm talking with my eyes closed now.

"I was angry that you were with Mace," she whispers.

"I told you I would have backed off if I knew you liked him, I barely knew him." It's a lot of work to open my eyes, but I do it and look over at her, "you said that wasn't the reason before."

"It wasn't! How are you so thick?" *Well that's just offensive.* Gabs lets out a little scream of frustration, "I didn't want him, I wanted you!" she buries her face in her hands, her shoulders heaving with silent sobs.

"Oh. *Oh...Ohhhh.*" I feel slow and stupid.

"Yeah." Gabs whispers.

Hammock Two, Laurel Zero

T rey

It's a little after midnight. I'm just passing time, reading some news, thinking about Laurel. I hope they're figuring their shit out, it seems like a waste to lose the friendship. Ollie has been asleep by my feet on the bed, but she suddenly perks up, staring out the window. Right after she does, I hear a noise outside. At first I think it might be some kind of animal, but then I hear voices.

Leaving the bedroom lamp on so I don't startle them, I quietly walk out into the living room where I can look out the window without being seen in the darkness. It's Gabs and Laurel, arms linked, standing near the hammock. The window is open and their voices carry clearly.

"Shhhh. Shhhh. Shhhh!" Laurel has her finger over her mouth as she tries to get Gabs to stop giggling.

"Oh-kayyyy sorry sorry," Gabs giggles.

Finding My Sun

"So I had a bad experience with this thing and I want to get it right," Laurel points at the hammock. "If I wasn't still kinda mad I would give you all the details, but let's just leave it there."

"Want me to hold it still?" Gabs giggles, taking hold of the edge of the hammock.

"Maybe that would work," Laurel turns around and carefully backs up to the edge of the hammock. She sits on it and then leans back, but instead of turning she just dangles her head over the other side.

"I don't think that's right," Gabs giggles, she puts an arm under Laurel's legs as if she's going to help her turn."Here, lift up your feet so you can la-" Laurel shrieks as the hammock does a complete flip and she lands on her belly in the sand.

"Well *that* wasn't right," Gabs says thoughtfully as Laurel rolls to her back and lays there, gasping and laughing.

"Here, try putting your knee on there while I hold it," Gabs moves to the edge and Laurel holds a finger up in the air.

"No, no, no, *that* has already been attempted," Laurel wags her hand back and forth. She holds up both of her hands and Gabs pulls her to her feet. They stand, swaying for a moment, before they walk over and sit on the edge of the deck together.

"Do you think you could try?" Gabs whispers.

"I wouldn't really know where to start," Laurel's voice is sad.

I'm not sure where the conversation took a turn, but they look at each other and touch foreheads.

"You could kiss me," Gabs whispers. *Wait, what?*

"I don't think that's how it works," Laurel whispers back.

"One kiss. If you don't feel anything, I'll let it go," Gabs stands, pulling Laurel up to face her, "just so I know."

Laurel stares at Gabs for a long moment.

"Okay." Laurel says softly, her expression solemn.

88

Laurel closes her eyes, standing still. Gabs reaches out and cups Laurel's face gently in both hands, stepping close, their bodies touching. She looks like she's moving in slow motion as she ever so slowly touches her lips to Laurel's. One of her hands slides down Laurel's arm and around her waist, the other hand moves behind her neck, holding her tight.

It's a pretty epic kiss.

I realize I'm standing there, staring out the window, at what is supposed to be a private moment. Turning quietly, I walk back to my bedroom.

* * *

Not long after, I hear the door from the deck click open and I can see Laurel in the moonlight as she comes through my bedroom doorway. She strips off her clothes, letting them fall to the floor.

"Trey? Are you awake?" She asks softly.

"Yes."

Laurel walks to the bed. I lift the blankets, inviting her in. She crawls on the bed and snuggles into my side, her head on my chest. Once she's settled she gives a little sigh.

"Are you okay?" I lean down and kiss the top of her head.

"I...will be," she gives a sad little hiccup. I hold her close, wondering if she's falling asleep. Her breathing evens out and I can feel her relaxing. It surprises me when I hear her voice again, soft, near sleep.

"I love...her, but...you."

It's Complicated

❧❧❧

*L*aurel

"Are there no clouds in this part of the freaking earth?"

I groan, as I roll over, trying to cover up my face with the blankets and ignore the insistent demands of my bladder. Trey laughs as he walks over to the closet, pulling on a shirt and shorts.

"*Usually* the lack of clouds is the appeal. Feeling a little delicate this morning?" He walks over to the bed and sits on the edge, smoothing my hair back from my face. "Do you want something to eat?"

"No, that would be really awesome, but I'd better get back to the house, I think Gabs stayed in my room last night. Things got…complicated." *So very complicated. Also, I think I fell off the hammock again.*

"Yeah you kind of mentioned that last night." He sounds casual, but I freeze at his words. I don't really remember

90

talking to him last night, just crawling in bed and going to sleep. *Ohmygod what did I tell him?*

"Did I? Um…what all did I tell you?" Sitting up, I immediately regret it as my head starts a dull pounding. Trey looks uncomfortable, *ohmygod what did I say to him? Is he blushing?*

He is, a slow blush is creeping up his neck and he runs a hand through his dark hair. His eyes meet mine and he sighs.

"Okay I don't want you to think I'm a creep, I only went to the window because I heard a noise." *Well fuck me sideways, he saw me with Gabs. He's probably six shades of weirded out.* "Anyway… it looked like you two were…figuring stuff out," he concludes softly.

"I don't even know why we came over here last night," *that's a lie, I wanted to see if I could get in the hammock because drunk me felt like a superhero.* "I knew I wanted to see you, I'm so sorry it got so complicated…did I…say anything else?" He shrugs it off, not making eye contact.

"Nah, you were pretty tired by then, that was about it." *'About', oh no, what else did I say?* Trey turns and heads for the doorway, "I'm going to go out and grab a few waves before they die down."

"Um, okay, so I'll see you later?" My stomach has a nervous flutter, I hate this feeling.

"Sure, later." Trey walks out to the kitchen and a moment later I hear him leave the house. *Sure is the 'no' of yes's.*

Dragging myself out of bed, I locate my clothes and get dressed, feeling like I've been run over by a truck. I don't know how to deal with Trey now, I feel bad that he saw Gabs kiss me, but it was what she needed to let go of this idea that we can be together. The kiss was nice, she was a very good kisser, but it didn't 'awaken' a damn thing, I'm straight.

Gabs was disappointed and hurt, thinking maybe I should try

harder. She seems to think I'm ignoring some latent impulse out of spite. I was sad, but at the same time I feel positive that we can heal. We just need to take some time, acknowledge our shit and figure out our new normal. Gabs and I will come out the other side of this still friends.

I walk out into the sand and stand in the trees for a while, watching Trey. He's paddled out pretty far, just sitting on his board, riding the swells. I hope he still wants to take off for a while, sail around the islands. Maybe he just needed a little time to himself too. I wave at him and it's gratifying when he lifts a hand in response.

Gabs is sitting at the table with Margo when I walk up on their deck. She gives me a sad little smile. Margo stands, taking both of their mugs to the kitchen.

"I'm going to meet Babe at the market, Laurel," Margo calls, "we'll see you later, okay?" She waits to hear me agree and then walks out of the house. I hear the buzz of the motorbike as she rides away. I sit across the table from Gabs, feeling awkward.

"Did you wake up bi?" Gabs tries for the joke.

"Not today," I give up a little laugh, shrugging.

"So you're saying there's a chance?" She grins at me.

"Gabs, I don't want you to live your life waiting for something that's not happening." My voice is soft, but firm. I hate to make the smile fade right back off her face, but I can't be what she needs, I don't love her the way she wants me to and it hurts.

"I know," she whispers. Standing from the table, she looks out at the water for a moment.

"I'm going to take a few days on a different island, reset, get my head straight before I go back to the city," she announces suddenly, turning back to me.

"It's a beautiful place," I agree, "keep in touch, don't go in your shell over this, Gabs."

"No shell," she nods, "I'll talk to you when you come back, I need time."

"I don't know if I'm coming back, Gabs. I didn't like the person I was in the city, I wasn't paying attention to what *I* needed." I can't find the right words, and she looks upset.

"You didn't like the person you were? How does that work exactly? What else do you need?" Gab's yells, suddenly furious. "I'm trying to give you everything, Laurel, I love you!"

"Me not wanting to go back to the city has nothing to do with you, Gabs," I whisper sadly. "This is not about you. This is about me. I was going through the motions there, just existing," I shrug, unsure how to explain when she has no intention of really listening anyway. "There's got to be more out in this world for me. I want to be open to the chance, I don't want to be afraid of my life anymore."

"Is that why you dove into the arms of another star?" Gabs snaps, "Because you're afraid of your life? What the fuck does that even mean?"

"What the hell are you talking about?!" *This conversation is all over the place.*

"You took all of a week to be sleeping with Trey Blake." She folds her arms over her chest and stares at me. "My god, Laurel, do you even know who he is?"

"You can't be angry at me for moving on to a new relationship, Gabs. You can fuck off with that judgey tone, also." *Not sure who the hell she thinks she is right now...*

"*Whatever*." Gabs is in full-on bitch mode now. "It's not *my* fault you need a *man* to make your life complete." Turning, she walks down to my room, I hear her moving about, packing, as I sit there in disbelief. After a moment, my disbelief turns to anger and I stomp down the hall.

"*For your information,* I don't *need* a man."

Gabs ignores me, tossing a shirt into her suitcase and zipping it shut angrily.

"Maybe I hadn't heard of Trey before we met, is that such a bad thing?" *She's making me out to be some kind of pathetic loser that can't function without a man. I don't like it at all.* "We met and hit it off and I like him, it's that simple. I like him a lot."

"Yeah, I get it, a hottie walks by and winks at you and it's game on," Gabs huffs out a huge sigh, grabbing her phone. "I'm calling a cab, you do you, Boo."

"I can't just flip a switch and start banging you!" That came out as more of a shriek than I'd planned. *Tactless but accurate, wow, Laurel.*

"Well I can't just flip a switch and grow a dick!" Gabs fires back. We stare at each other for a long minute, breathing hard.

"In the movies we would both laugh and everything would be okay right now." I offer, feeling confused and upset.

"I think I need some time," Gabs sighs, "I don't feel like laughing yet."

"I don't feel like laughing either." I murmur.

"Goodbye, Laurel." Gabs picks up a small suitcase and shoulders her purse, turning towards the door.

"Goodbye, Gabrielle." I watch her, refusing to let a single tear roll down my cheek until she closes the door softly behind her as she leaves. I walk to my room, throw myself on the bed and stare up at the fan, watching it swirl lazily. It feels like the thing to do would be to have a good cry, but I'm too damn tired. I feel one tear roll down my temple into my hair, but that's all. I'm too wrung out for more.

As I lay here thinking, Gab's parting shots about Trey cycle through my brain. I wonder what he's doing…if he still wants to see me. I realize now that based on what he *said*, along with what he probably *saw*, he might not know *exactly* what happened last night.

Sitting up, I reach over and grab my laptop off the side table, scooting up until my back is against a pillow on the headboard. Flipping it open, I log in and open a search bar. Hesitating for just a second, I slowly type in Trey Blake.

Scrolling through slowly, I feel my heart drop. Not because he's a champion surfer…*that* is actually amazing and wonderful. According to the analysts and commentators, he's in line to take the number one spot across the board this year. I watch a couple of clips from last year, even spotting Brian in several of them.

What makes my heart drop is the pictures of Trey on the red carpet last year. He's famous. He's dated famous. He's been photographed all over the world. Surfing, going to clubs, smiling with fans. *And here I handed him some surfing photos like he's never seen himself surfing before…sheesh.*

Maybe things have moved too fast. I mean, I *am* seriously considering taking off on a trip around the islands with him and I barely know him. *I just jumped in with both feet and a heart held together with duct tape.*

Setting the laptop aside, I scoot down in the bed, hugging a pillow, determined to sleep until my life makes sense. *Battered as it feels, my heart still wants Trey.*

I wake up, disoriented, unsure if I've slept for a couple of hours or a couple of days. On a positive note, my hangover is gone. Climbing out of bed, I start stripping as I walk to the shower, grabbing my toothbrush on the way.

That Was...Surprising

T rey

    I'm just kicking around my house, wasting time. I don't know where Laurel and I stand, *also, I'm not sure I want to find out.* Ollie yowls at the door to be let out. I open it, walking out on the deck myself. The ocean's calm this afternoon, lapping at the shore. Stepping off the deck, I walk along the beach, heading for the rock where I first saw Laurel.

    She's there, sitting on the rock, arms wrapped around her knees. The edge of her dress flutters around her feet in the breeze as she stares at the water. When I get close, she notices me, her dark eyes finding mine. She watches me walk up without saying a word. I stop in front of her, wishing I knew what to say.

    My brain's best options so far consist of: *Hey, so are you going to be dating women now? And, do you still want to be with me? Smooth...very smooth, Brain.* I settle for safety.

"Hey," *shut up, that's all I've got.*

"Hey," her smile makes my chest tighten, *in a good way, not the heart attack way.*

"Where's your friend?" *Not very subtle but I'm going with it.* Laurel's eyebrows draw together unhappily. *Well shit.*

"She's gone, I think she was going to stay on another island for a while and then head back to the city." Laurel glances at me and then looks out at the water, shrugging her shoulders with a sigh. "Gabs is my friend and I love her, but she wanted more than I could give," she laughs softly, "you saw that much the other night."

"That was...surprising," I admit slowly.

"I bet it was," she chuckles, "anyway, I was hoping I would see you, I know I left things kind of weird."

"I wanted to see you too." Movement up the beach catches my eye. I can see someone walking towards us, it looks like a man in jeans and a dark t-shirt. Laurel turns to see what I'm looking at, squinting in the sun. We both watch him walk closer and suddenly she gasps.

"Mace?"

I Think You Broke My Brain

*L*aurel

"Hey, Love," his tone is breezy, like we're running into each other in a coffee shop back home. *What the crap?*

"Don't 'Hey, Love' me, what are you doing here?" I'm so confused right now. *Why would he come all this way when his last communication was a tepid-at-best apology via text?*

"Hi, I'm Mace, you look familiar." Mace walks over to Trey, holding out a hand. Trey shakes it, glancing at me.

"Mace Carson, right? Yeah dude, Trey Blake, we were both at Tahiti Pro last year, you did a set at one of the after parties." And they know each other, *because, of course they do.*

"Right, right, good to see you man! How's this season looking?" *What the crap heck is happening here, Mace knows and speaks surfing? Am I the only one that was apparently living under a rock?* They continue talking for a couple of minutes as I stand there speechless. *There are so many things wrong with this, let's start with, why is Mace here? This would be quite a trip for a not-happening-have-you-lost-your-mind booty call...*

"Ahem-hem!" I fake clear my throat loudly, startling them both, "sorry to break up the reunion, but I'm still not sure what's going on here." Mace looks at me guiltily, *yep, jilted girlfriend still standing here, jackass.*

"Shit, sorry, Lov-Laurel," Mace tosses me a smile and then looks at Trey. "Hey man, you cool if Laurel and I take a beat? We need to talk." Trey looks at me, his eyes serious.

"Sure. Laurel are you good with that?"

No. I nod yes.

"Okay, later then?" He waits for me to agree and heads across the beach. Mace and I sit silently for a moment, watching him go. Finally I huff out a sigh, waiting for him to speak.

"I should have called you," Mace stares at his hands as he speaks. "I should have followed you out the door that day." He comes over and sits on the rock beside me, looking at the water. "I was a selfish asshole. You deserved better." His eyes meet mine, "I'm sorry, Laurel." *Oof, right in the feels this guy.*

I'm not even torn. He was a blip in my life, a few months. It was fun, we had some good times, he completely fucked it up, it ended. I have no interest in trying to work things out, we didn't have that kind of connection. *The kind of connection I had instantly with Trey.* What I *don't* understand is why Mace wants to talk about this in the first place. He sent me a lame apology text, matter closed.

"All true," I say slowly, "but I don't know what to do with all of that now. I don't have anything left to give you, Mace." I watch his face, curious about where he's going with this conversation.

"You could give me your blessing...and you could help me...find Gabrielle," he says softly, finally meeting my eyes.

Ohmygod...he didn't come all this way to find me...he came to find Gabs...

"She wouldn't talk to me back home, just too riddled with guilt, I suppose," Mace prattles on, unaware that I'm about to spontaneously combust. "It's amazingly lucky that I found out she came this far, she happened to leave her email logged in when I went to her apartment to find her and I saw that she'd bought a plane ticket." He scoffs as if this is *such* an inconvenience.

"Have you seen her? Is she here?" Mace ends boldly and then looks at me, pulling away slightly as if becoming aware for the first time that he's being a world class dick who might be in imminent danger of grievous bodily harm.

I wasn't aware that I had a line in the sand before this moment. As it turns out, I do.

"Did you just hear a 'pop'?" I slide off the rock and turn to look at Mace, who looks around, confused. "No? Just me? Oh, probably only *I* could hear it because it was my brain. You *literally just popped my brain* you twat!" I am suddenly, completely, laughably, angry. Turning, I storm off down the beach, ranting and waving my arms like a crazy woman.

"Oh Laurel, I'm *soooo* sorry, I was a jerk, I should have *asked* before I slept with your best friend! *That* was my only mistake. Gah!" I turn back to see Mace, still sitting on the rock, watching me as if I'm a rabid fan and he might need protection.

"I mean it's not like I wanted you back," I continue, pointing an accusing finger at him, "but for one second my ego needed the teeny-tiny boost that you were sorry and you're NOT. You just want to find her again! Well fine! Go find her! She's on a different island, mad at *me* for not turning into a bisexual to make *her* happy! How's *that* for irony!?" Turning toward the water, I sit down in the sand, wrapping my arms around my knees. I don't care what Mace does, I kind of hope he just goes away.

No such luck, I hear the scrape of fabric on rock as he climbs down and then his shadow moves across the sand as he walks over and sits down beside me. We're both silent for several minutes. *Clearly I gave him a lot to process.*

"She, huh…and you, like you and her, huh, so…" *I think Mace's brain popped too.* He tries again.

"Gabrielle, um, she, not me. Huh…Pbbbt." Mace gives up and blows a big raspberry.

"Yeah, a mouth-fart is probably an accurate summation of this situation," I nod sagely, cracking an only-slightly-crazed smile. *I mean really, what else is there to do?*

"Oh, *come* on," I glower, standing up and dusting sand off the back of my dress, "You're going to buy me a sangria." Mace stares at me for a long moment and stands, looking a little dazed. He pulls himself together with some effort.

"Fair enough, I'd love one, but I think I have some questions."

"Fair enough." I walk up the beach to Margo's, my confused rock star ex trailing behind me.

I Guess That's... That

*T*rey

It's been hours since I walked away from Laurel and Mace on the beach. I'm laying in the hammock, feeling like a dumbass. There I was, *having a conversation about surfing,* with Laurel's ex. He asked to talk to her and I just walked away. I mean, what was I supposed to do, refuse? He came all the way to the island, clearly he wants to patch things up. If she wants to go back to him, that's her decision. *But it hurts to know that's a possibility.*

Mace Carson. Not even close to the type I would have guessed Laurel would date. Not because he's a legit A-lister. More because he's a rock star, which just doesn't seem like her scene. *She belongs on the beach, wind in her hair, a camera in her hand.* Tired of my own thoughts, I stand up and get my motorcycle out of the garage. Kicking it to life, I drive the island highway for a while, thinking.

The other night when she was falling asleep, *and, to be fair, drunk,* Laurel said something about love and her and…you. My brain will not let go of this, arguing back and forth what Laurel meant, *and more importantly who?*

I'd assumed 'her' was Gabrielle, which seems to be the case. I'd *hoped* 'you' was me, *assuming she remembered where she was and that she was with me.* I'm now starting to think 'you' has an equal chance of being Mace. I'm also starting to think that even if she's not making up with Mace as I sit on this motorcycle, *torturing myself with a circular conversation,* she might not actually be ready for a relationship with me.

* * *

Maybe Laurel needs time to decide what, *and who* she wants. She just broke up with Mace. She just sort-of lost her best friend. I didn't know any of that when I saw her sitting on the rock that day. I just knew I saw a beautiful woman, with vibrant red hair, sitting on a rock by the ocean and I understood what the old stories about a 'siren's call' meant. I couldn't have left Laurel alone if I'd been offered the crown jewels to walk away.

I've dated, but nothing serious since college, *when I thought Rebecca Tucker was 'the one' until she revealed her grand plan to start popping out babies as soon as we both graduated...she wanted six.* There was no shortage of options at the competitions, but right after college, all I did was surf. I started climbing the ranks, gaining points. I traveled everywhere the waves were, surfing, winning.

Things changed when my agent, Donnie, got me an endorse-ment deal for a line of board shorts a while back. The money was insane and it was basically a modelling gig. At first there were a few calls…then there were a lot. Donnie wouldn't stop calling me the 'flavor of the month'. He was so damn excited when I was cast in a minor role, *as a surfer,* for a movie. He thought it was our big break. I moved to L.A. for a few months, did the movie, even dated one of the stars.

The movie did well, but my heart wasn't in acting or modeling or any of it, really. I wanted the sand and the waves, just me and a board. I *hated* the red carpet. I felt like a trained monkey in a suit whenever I walked by all the flashing cameras.

One night I walked the carpet and just kept walking, ditched my date, got back in the car and left. Went to my folk's house in Florida, bought my house on St. Lamoix a couple weeks later. Called Donnie after a week. He was about to put out a missing person report on me.

Donnie damn near dropped me completely when I told him I was serious about leaving. I don't care about fame, but if it happens, I don't want to be famous for anything but surfing.

It was actually really cool that Laurel didn't know who I was when we met. I didn't have to wonder if she was only interested because I'm considered some kind of celebrity. Meeting her felt right, but maybe she needs some time. I thought every damn thing clicked tight the second I met her, she's smart and funny, adventurous.

The more I think about it, maybe I just wanted everything to fit. Hell, I don't even know how long she's planning to stay. She might be heading back to her city life any day now, just took a break in the islands to reset…it happens a lot.

I'm terrible company and I'm tired of thinking. Turning the bike around, I head for Margo's. Fifteen minutes later, I pull in the lot and park the bike around the side of the building. I walk around to the beach side of the bar so I can just step up on the deck, then I freeze.

Laurel and Mace are sitting at the bar, their backs to me. As I watch, he puts an arm around her and she leans her head on his shoulder. He kisses her hair. *And that's, that.* Turning away before anyone notices, I get back on the bike, kick it to life and go home.

I stay home long enough to grab the shit I packed earlier and head for my boat. I stow everything and then just sit on the deck, staring up at the moon. I'm disappointed Laurel would go back to Mace that easily. He must have had the right words. I keep picturing them, sitting together, his lips pressed to her hair.

"Well...it's done. She was never really mine anyway." I say the words out loud to the moon, staring at it until I let the slow rocking of the boat lull me into a fake sense of peace. Heading down to the cabin, I go to bed. I can smell her perfume, lingering on the pillows. It's a long time before I sleep.

Dissecting the Rhombus

L aurel

"So she slept with me...because she was mad at you...for sleeping with me, instead of her?" Mace is so confused, especially when he's had five glasses of sangria. *I've learned my lesson, I'm nursing my second glass until the end of the night.*

"Well, in a nutshell, yes." I agree. We've gone over it a few times now and he's having a moment, this is quite a big rattle to the cage where he hides his fairly fragile ego.

"And you...turned her down...because you're not bi," he continues slowly.

"Right." *This is getting old.*

"And there's no chance that..." *He got on a reconciliation tangent after his third glass.*

"No." I keep my voice gentle, but, *ugh, enough already.*

"Well. Okay." Mace stirs his sangria with his finger, trying to fish out a piece of fruit. He looks at me, his face serious.

"You know," he begins, stopping to eat the fruit he managed to catch and chewing reflectively, "when we met I wondered why you were interested. I could tell it wasn't the groupie thing, you're not the type."

"Hmm, thanks?"

He waves this off in a 'you know what I meant' kind of way.

"No, really, what was it? I haven't figured it out and I think that when Gabrielle and I got drunk that night and…well you know how that ended…"

It's my turn to flap my hand in a 'yep, moving on' kind of way.

"Well the thing is, I think we were both afraid of disappointing you? So the more we talked the more it became a self-fulfilling prophecy?" He stares at me hard, I can almost see his brain working as he tries to will himself sober. "Does that make sense? We got to talking and I think the one thing we had in common was that neither of us felt good enough for you." He reaches a sangria-sticky finger over and boops me on the nose as I stare at him, shocked.

"How in the crap did you come to *that* conclusion?" I wheeze out, surreptitiously wiping off my nose.

"It's not rocket science, Love." Mace teases, resting his elbow on the table and propping his chin on his hand. "You're fucking *amazing*. You see the world differently, constantly challenging the people around you just by being so bloody brilliant. You write these ridiculously intelligent things and take these phenomenal pictures and you know who *you* are. No one has to tell you, because you *know.* You know?" Mace nods a few too many times in support of his point and then jerks as his chin falls off his hand. He smiles at me, clasping his hands around his glass instead.

"Well, I bu-, no, huh?" I stammer, because I'm confused and flattered...and confused. *Let's try that again.*

"Well, I don't even know what to do with all of that. I don't feel like I'm amazing," I whisper. "I feel like I'm on a train with no brakes half the time and I don't want to miss anything. The other half of the time I feel like I'm crawling through life missing *everything*." I shake my head because I don't know if that even makes sense, but it's all I've got for words.

Staring at Mace for a second, I think, *really* think, about the day we met. He stares back gravely, waiting.

"I stopped and spoke to you that day because you were unexpected." I pause, remembering. "There we were, in the middle of a huge party. I heard your voice as I walked down a back hall, looking for the toilets. On my way back, I stopped and listened for a little bit. You were sitting there by the service door, smoking, talking to this waiter." I can tell by Mace's expression that he remembers.

"You and the waiter were talking about a book he was reading on his break. It was one that you'd read before and you were having a little impromptu book club meeting, right there on the steps." I bump my shoulder into Mace's, he smiles.

"I remember, his name was Connor. The book was...*The Eagle Has Landed*," Mace agrees.

"Well, that's why you *were* good enough," I shrug. "*That's* why I was interested. I wanted to meet you because everyone else was partying it up and you randomly decided that you'd rather talk about a book, with a guy you'd never met. That just struck me as really cool." I take a sip of my drink.

"I want you to know, *that* is the best thing anyone has *ever* said to me," Mace announces seriously, a pleased smile on his face. "See Laurel, that's why you're amazing. Most people I date like the lifestyle, the money, the voice, blah blah blah blah barf." He stares at me for a minute. "You saw something else."

"I did," I agree, sipping my sangria.

"And what do you see in Trey?" He surprises me and I spend a moment coughing sangria out of my lungs.

"Well...he's free." I shrug, trying to figure out how to describe someone I like to someone I used to like. "I saw him the first day I was here. He was surfing and I took some pictures and all I could think was he was just free, flying across the water. He came here to the bar that night, we met and I just..." the words fail me at this point. Mace waits patiently for me to continue.

"I feel seen when I'm with Trey," I whisper. "He makes me feel equal, like he's as lucky to be with me as I am with him..." I can't look at Mace, it's too hard, I don't know what else to say. *I examine my cuticles as if I'm due on set for a hand commercial, just hoping he'll break the silence.*

"I'm sorry I didn't give you that, Laurel," Mace sighs. "I would hate...after all of this...if we could not be friends."

"I think we can work on being friends," I agree. Mace puts an arm around me and I lean my head against his shoulder, emotionally exhausted. I feel his lips in my hair for just a moment and he gives me a squeeze.

"Then, as your friend, I'm telling you that you need to go see where things lead with Trey. Go be *seen*. I know it makes me a complete ass, but I fucked things up with you because it was too much, I thought you expected too much. I know that wasn't fair, I wanted it to be your fault, but it was all mine." Mace gives me another side hug before releasing me, picking up his sangria and motioning to the bartender for another.

I really want to be offended and angry. I want to hate Mace. He slept with my best friend. But I can't lie and say that it doesn't make me feel good that in some way he found me too 'amazing' to handle. I mean, I realize that could be a tremendous line of crap he's feeding me, but I'm going to take it. I don't want to fight with him, he's not mine, I don't think he ever really was, if I'm honest.

As Mace sits there, sucking down another glass of sangria, I think about what I want to tell him. Also I can't resist one tiny little dig, my ego kind of demands it at this point.

"Mace, I've got to say that I'm glad you came here, because it helps me say goodbye to us. I'm mostly going to remember you as a harmless idiot...no offense." Mace laughs out loud and shakes his head, taking a drink of the sangria that the bartender places in front of him. "That said," I continue, "I don't think you should chase after Gabs. She needs some time and space." I look at Mace earnestly, hoping he'll take me seriously. He stares at me for a long minute before nodding slowly.

"Yes, the fair Gabrielle needs to find her own way. My ego is bruised but I will recover without her affection." Mace gestures dramatically and I giggle. He picks up his sangria and I hear another giggle echoing behind me. We turn at the same time to see a pretty blonde with tan legs for miles, in short shorts and a bandeau top. She's practically vibrating out of her strappy sandals with excitement.

"Are you Mace Carson?" She bubbles. And, just like that, Mace flips the switch to rock star.

"You got me Love, and who might you be?" Tossing me a wink, Mace gives her 'the grin' and takes a big drink of sangria.

"Yay!" She claps her hands with excitement, *claps her hands for fuckssake, ugh.* "I'm Cassie and my friends and I thought it was you, do you think we could take a picture?" She glances at me, "Is this your...girlfriend?" *Wow, Cassie has a really good 'get dead' look, yikes.*

"No, he's all yours, Cassie," I keep my voice sweet, *but I roll my eyes at her because, Bitch, please.* "We were just catching up. I'm going to head out soon anyway."

"I'll be over in a mo' sweets, let me finish talking to Laurel first." Mace continues to ooze charm and Cassie absorbs it like she lives in a pineapple under the sea.

"You betcha!" She gives him a little finger wave before bouncing back to her table where her friends are waiting excitedly.

"As your new friend, you'd tell me if I shouldn't leave you alone, right?" Mace gives me a sly look as he grins.

"As our new-found friendship is in its mere *infancy*, I'd say less is more and you should go entertain that pretty blonde wolfpack over there." I smile back and we both laugh.

"You take care, Laurel," Mace gives me a hug.

"You make sure that girl is *at least* 22 or it's weird, Mace," I tease, hugging him back. He saunters over to Cassie's table and it gets a lot noisier. I turn back to the bar as Margo walks out of the kitchen.

"Everything okay, Chica?" She pours herself a glass of sangria and settles on the stool next to me with a sigh.

"You know what? I think everything is actually really good." I smile, raising my glass in a little toast. She clinks the rim of hers to mine.

"Cheers to really good, Chica."

We chat for a while and the bar eventually starts to empty. Cassie's friends deserted her for the dance floor after a while and then left, but she and Mace are still at the table. He's been pounding the drinks pretty hard. I'm not surprised when I hear him singing. He belts out a few phrases of one of his major songs to Cassie's delight. She sits there, hands clasped under her chin, starry eyed.

"You sing to me like that every night and I'll follow you to the ends of the earth, Sugar." I hear Cassie breathe the words, sultry as all get-out.

"How about we start with you helping me get back to my hotel, Love," Mace smiles drunkenly. "The ends of the earth can wait until tomorrow." They walk out of the bar, arms around each other's waists, propping each other up as they saunter drunkenly down the boardwalk.

"Well I'll be damned," Margo starts laughing. I glance at her, wondering what she's laughing about. She nods her head at Cassie and Mace.

"Cassie is the waitress that quit because her horoscope said so, I guess it was right about that millionaire after all." I stare after them and then Margo and I laugh until we cry.

What Kind of Coffee Is This?

T rey

It's raining when I wake up, a soothing sound as the drops hit the deck above. Stretching, I get up and pull on some shorts and a hoodie. May as well go up and make sure everything is secure in case the wind picks up, check the weather radar and see how long this is going to last. Running my hand over my jaw, I'm thinking about coffee and a shave as I walk up the stairs. I'm surprised to find one of those things waiting for me.

Laurel is sitting on the deck under a large umbrella, two take out cups sitting by her knee. She gives me an uncertain smile, picking up one of the cups and holding it out to me.

"Good morning," she says softly. "I'm glad you didn't leave before I got a chance to see you." I reach out and take the cup from her hand. Our fingers brush and I'm pissed I'm going to miss out on the chance with Laurel. *Stupid rock star and his stupid words that gets him the woman I want for myself.*

"Good morning to you, too," I raise the cup at her briefly in thanks, "here I am." She blushes, dropping her head and fiddling with the zipper pull on her jacket. Good. I have no intention of making it easy for her to tell me that she chose him over me.

"I don't know how you take yours," she points at my cup, clearly making small talk.

"This is fine, thanks." I pause, thinking, then decide to fire the first shot before I lose my nerve. "Although since you told me how your last break up went, this has a definite sense of irony." *Your move, Girl, time to rip off the bandaid.* Laurel looks down at her cup and then stares at mine, upset.

"I didn't bring you break up coffee!" She exclaims. "I mean, wait, are you saying you're breaking up with me and we have coffee?" She pauses, taking a deep breath. "Wait…were we *in* a relationship?"

"No, it was nothing, don't worry about it," *now I feel like an idiot*, I mean we hadn't actually *defined* anything about us, but we did have an amazing night on the boat together. I guess I hoped we were official enough at that point. All I wanted was more of her, I can't believe I read the whole situation so wrong.

"It didn't feel like nothing to me," Laurel says in a low voice, one solitary tear slides down her cheek and almost breaks me.

"Then why did you let it go so easily?" My throat feels tight. She stares at me.

"I've let everything *but* you go, Trey," Laurel whispers, "Look, I'm sorry I put so much on you, I guess I didn't realize I had that much baggage when we met." She shrugs, taking a drink of her coffee, "I met you and I didn't want to deal with anything else, I just wanted to get to know *you*. Everything else seemed sad and dumb and unimportant. You felt like the sun, shining just for me," dashing away the tear on her cheek with a careless swipe of her hand, Laurel falls silent.

"Did you come here this morning to tell me you're leaving with Mace?" It finally occurs to me that maybe I've missed something important. *The incredulous look Laurel is giving me right now confirms this possibility.*

"Why on earth would I leave with Mace?" She stares at me with wide eyes, utterly confused. *Yep, I missed something.*

"Because you guys were very cozy at the bar last night when I came looking for you…and now I think maybe I should have stayed longer to watch that play out?" Laurel's mouth forms a surprised 'O' for a moment and then she blurts out a laugh.

"I wish you would have, he put on quite a show," she shakes her head. "Oh, this is such a mess, Trey."

"How about you just tell me the story, fill in the gaps?" I offer. Laurel smiles.

"How about I tell you over breakfast? You're soaking wet." It's true, and I didn't even notice. The rain is light, but it has soaked my hoodie and there are drops falling off the ends of my hair.

"Fair enough," I nod, smiling back. Turning, I walk down the steps and pull out some dry clothes and a towel. Pulling off the hoodie, I throw the towel over my head, rubbing to dry my hair a little bit. As I drop it down around my neck, I feel Laurel's hands slide around my waist. She kisses a spot between my shoulder blades and I groan, turning and capturing her face in my hands. Our lips meet and this kiss is everything I couldn't say. Her lips move against mine, warm and demanding. This is anything *but* nothing, she is everything.

Her hands find the waist of my shorts and she shoves them

off my hips, her body pinning me between us. Her hands slide up my chest and she pushes lightly, her lips still moving against mine. I take the hint and sit on the bed, finding the waist of her pants and popping the button. Sliding my hands up her ribs, I pull away from her long enough to get her shirt up and over her head before I'm kissing her again. *I love these damn bras she wears that aren't really bras just bits of lace with no hooks, fucking hot.*

Laurel shoves her pants off her hips and kicks them off, bringing her knees up on either side of my hips, straddling me. She grinds our hips together and I want to drive in deep.

"Condom," I break away from Laurel's lips just long enough to look up at her face. Her cheeks are flushed, her lips swollen. She nods, leaning to reach in the side table drawer as I kiss my way down her shoulder, nipping her with my teeth. She gasps and hums her pleasure before sitting back, straddling my thighs as I hold her hips steady.

My eyes want to roll back as she rolls the condom down my length and then she rears up. I feel her heat right before she takes me in one stroke. Leaning back on my elbows, I slowly pump up into her as she finds her rhythm, her hips rolling. Her hands find my ribs and I feel the bite of her nails as she moves faster, looking down at me.

"Fuckkkk Girl," I gasp, fighting the urge to flip her over and pound into her, I let her set the pace. She smiles, moving faster, grinding our bodies together with every roll of her hips. Her eyes slide closed and she moves even faster, a moan escaping her lips. I feel her rhythm falter and her head drops back as she clenches around me, trying to keep her hips rolling.

When she takes a gasping breath, I reach up, pulling her to my chest as I roll us. Holding my weight up off of her, I start moving, slow as long as I can and then pounding her as I feel that heavy weight building in my gut. When I change the angle she lets out a strangled cry.

"Yes, there, hard, yes!"

I speed up, pounding her hard right over that spot, again and again, until her nails dig into my back and she arches off the bed under me with a scream. I come with her, driving deep and holding her tight.

So, we missed breakfast. *Fine, we missed lunch too.*

That evening, sitting at my usual table at Margo's, Laurel fills in the gaps in the story.

"Let me get this straight, Mace was here to find *Gabrielle*?" I shake my head, dumbfounded. "I mean, she's pretty and all, but, well, she's not *you*." Laurel blushes, nodding, as I continue. "He also hit on you, you turned him down, you two managed to salvage some kind of friendship…and he left with Cassie the waitress?"

"*Ex* waitress," Margo cuts in with a laugh as she walks by on her way to the kitchen. "Make sure you tell him that part Laurel."

Hours later, Laurel and I walk along the beach, the music and lights fading in the distance. Turning back, I can see Margo's bar, the lights are dim and almost all of the customers have gone for the night. Margo and Williams are dancing, arms wrapped around each other as she smiles up at him. Laurel turns, following my gaze, giving a happy sigh as I pull her into a hug.

"Well, we've tried a couple times, but I think the third time will be a charm," I lean back a little, smiling down at her. "Laurel

Williams, will you go sailing with me?"

Livin' the Dream

aurel
4 months later

"Come on, come on, come on, you got it Girl, yes!" Trey's hands are strong around my thighs, his feet planted firmly on his board as I finally, *finally* hit my first knee stand on the water. I feel like I'm flying, just holding steady, feeling him control the board under us.

Heading back to the house as the waves die down and the heat of the day really sets in, I give Ollie a scratch between the ears as she twines around my legs. Trey stows the board on the rack and we head for the kitchen to make some lunch.

Life in the city feels so very far away now. I went back once, about three months ago, to sign off on my apartment and have everything packed and shipped. I visited Gabs, it was different, definitely cooler. It was disappointing, but I get it, she's protecting herself and I'm probably being unfair. I'm not

119

giving up on the idea of finding our way back to friendship, though.

When I got back to the island, I officially moved in with Trey. Ollie peed on two pairs of my shoes. It took a month *and several cans of tuna,* but she finally accepted me. Now I can't go to bed without her stalking up to my pillow and curling around the top of my head like a furry little dictator.

Trey has been teaching me to surf, causing me to thank my dad multiple times for the years of dance lessons that have suddenly paid off with excellent balance. *And also, a pretty decent level of graceful movement if I do say so myself.*

He has *not* successfully taught me how to get in that fucking hammock. *That* thing is possessed by some sort of disgruntled spirit and I give up on it.

"Take a look at this," Trey sets his laptop on the table between us, scrolling until he finds what he wants to show me. It's an exhibition on the Gold Coast, several of the features are tandem surfing.

"Oh perfect, that's right after League, Trey! Adding it to the list!" He laughs, watching me walk to the desk where I grab my battered planner.

He and Brian have been training like crazy and Trey is defending his title again this year. We've been planning a trip to celebrate. *Trey says we'll be celebrating the end of the insane training Brian forces him into, but I know we'll be celebrating his win.*

Trey has a long list of places he wants to show me, including a lot of new beaches to surf. This has played in extremely well with my blog, which has exploded. *Not gonna lie, I did a little shameless name dropping and there are a lot of pictures of Trey. He likes to tell everyone I get the 'exclusives' which is our code for 'let's go have a quickie'.*

I, in turn, have been busily getting Trey as addicted to photography as I am. A good chunk of the pictures on the blog are ones he has taken. I've got a new camera picked out for his birthday in a couple of weeks.

Pushing back from the table, he stands behind me as I write, sliding his arms around my waist and resting his chin on my shoulder.

"I love you, Girl." He rumbles, nuzzling my neck and nipping at my earlobe.

"I love you, too," I murmur, turning in his arms and tilting my face up for a kiss. I get a happy flutter in my belly every time he says the words. As his lips move with mine, his hands roam my body, tightening on my waist as he lifts me up and sits me on the counter. *Hmmmm, time for an exclusive? Yes, please.*

A Question in the Sand

*T*rey
6 months later

"Laurel, have you seen my camera?" I'm on the deck, watching the water and petting Ollie. Laurel just went in to grab us a couple of beers.

"Um, yeah, it's here on the desk, do you want it?" She's preoccupied, popping the caps off the beers.

"Yeah, bring it out here, could you? I want you to see some of the shots I got this morning."

"Sure thing," she walks back out, handing me the camera and a beer before sinking onto the couch next to me with a sigh. I turn the camera on, scroll around a minute and hand it to her nonchalantly.

"Take a look."

Laurel takes the camera from me and starts slowly flipping through the pictures I took this morning. A soft comment here and there, otherwise she's just looking, it's her habit to go through all of them first, then go back and analyze. *That's what I'm counting on today.*

I stand up and walk over to the table as if I'm getting something, listening carefully. I hear a soft gasp and I know she's reached the pictures I *really* wanted her to see. Pulling the ring out of my pocket, I silently drop to one knee and wait.

The last three pictures of the set are, "Laurel, Marry, Me?" written in the sand.

A moment later, Laurel dives in my arms, laughing through tears as she smothers me with kisses.

"Will you marry me, Girl?"

"Yes, Trey, *yes*." she smiles, eyes shining, right as Margo and Williams round the corner of the house. Laurel is sitting in my lap on the deck where she tackled me, holding out a trembling hand. I slip the ring on her finger and smile at them.

"Oh you two, sorry! We should have called," Margo looks back and forth between Laurel and I, then she spies the ring and starts flapping her hands in front of her eyes as if stopping herself from crying.

"No, no, perfect timing," I assure her, "I was just asking Laurel to be my wife."

"Ohmygod shut up!" Margo squeals. Giving up the battle, she lets the tears come, rushing over to hug Laurel. She excitedly oohs and ahhs over the ring and then hugs me as well.

"Look at that, it's amazing, you did such a good job, Trey!" Margo gushes. Laurel laughs and wraps her right arm around my waist as Margo continues to admire the ring.

"I love it, Trey, I've never seen anything like it," Laurel says softly.

"It's a Caribbean sunset," I explain, running a finger over the stones. There's a one-carat round center diamond, with five oval cut opals fanning out above it, all anchored to a delicate gold band. "My mother and my Grandma both wear them as their wedding rings too, it's kind of a tradition," I explain.

Margo sighs happily and then looks at Williams, who has been quiet since they walked up. Her eyes narrow.

"Babe, you don't seem too surprised," her tone is suspicious and as she walks over to him, he gives her a grin.

"Trey and I had a conversation almost two months ago regarding his worthiness to propose marriage to Laurel," Williams agrees in his formal way.

"Two months ago?" A lesser man would be wilting at her tone, but Williams is long practiced in disarming Margo.

"Indeed," he nods. "Once Trey and I established that he is eminently suitable from my perspective, we set the proviso that Laurel would have to reach the same conclusion," he pauses, leaning down to give Margo a quick kiss. "Shortly after, we summarily agreed that you, my love, would appreciate the element of surprise and the forthcoming realization that this gives you the opportunity to plan another wedding." Williams smiles as Margo's eyes widen.

"Oh, Babe, you're right! Ooooooo this is going to be so much fun! My first beach wedding!" Margo claps her hands, hugging Laurel excitedly. "You just leave everything to me! I'll have samples in a couple of days okay! This is going to be a-fucking-mazing!" Margo hops off the deck, heading around the corner of the house towards their car.

"Come on babe! I've got things to do!" She calls. Williams smiles, turning to us.

"I will do what I can to corral her," he promises solemnly. "Historically this has not been successfully completed, but I will be able to give you a few days to celebrate your new status as affianced."

"Thanks Dad," Laurel laughs, walking over and hugging him tightly.

"Let's *go* Babe!" Margo calls from the driveway.

"Of course, once her planning obsession reaches its apex, I would simply advise that you hold on tight and ride it out," Williams continues. "In Margo's words, 'it's on like *Donkey Kong*' at that point."

II

Part Two: A Beach Wedding

The Invitation

abrielle

G   I stare at the invitation in my hands, waiting for the feelings to hit my heart like a thousand needles. The cream colored paper is thick, classic, expensive, very fitting for the woman that for the better part of my life I have called my best friend.

Laurel is getting married.

My hand isn't even shaking. *Maybe this is what shock feels like*. I don't even dare to hope that the long months that have passed since I last saw her have numbed the pain. It probably helps that the envelope arrived almost a month ago. I knew what it was then, I just didn't want to open it and be right.

The tiniest spark of happiness lights up the dark recesses of my brain where I have stored my feelings for Laurel. That tiny spark is hopeful. Laurel found love and in a little more than one month she's getting married, not to me, *but maybe that means my someone is still out there.*

Setting the invitation on the counter, I move around the kitchen, the familiar act of grinding coffee and pouring it into the French press soothes me. Heat the water, pour it on the grounds, look out the window. Feed my fish, Trish. Check the weather. Push the plunger of the French press down slowly and pour that first delicious cup.

Anything to avoid thinking about that invitation sitting on my counter. Anything to avoid the war my emotions are currently having as I try to determine how I feel. Part of me wants to be so fucking happy for her that the tears are hot in my eyes. The other part is devastated at the concrete evidence that I'm alone, I've badly damaged our friendship and I've officially lost Laurel to someone else.

Flipping through the rest of the mail, I bin several advertisements, tuck a couple of bills in the file so I don't lose them and glance at the clock. Time to get downstairs and open the shop. I'm not the only one needing my caffeine fix this morning.

I can smell muffins baking as I step out of my apartment onto the landing, walking down two steep flights of stairs to the street. I live in a beautiful old building in the downtown historic district. My uncle owned a coin shop here for years while the area suffered through many phases of urban renovation. He sold the building to me when he retired four years ago, made me promise to keep it for a while. He was right, the area was ready.

In an explosion of boutiques, renovated hotels, a new casino and a landslide of new business flowing to the area, my uncle's old coin shop was suddenly at the corner of Busy and Booming.

The timing was perfect for me to open the coffee house that I'd always wanted. Street level is the coffee house, the second floor I've rented out to a very upscale tailor that has a steady stream of customers, and the third floor is my apartment.

My baker, Jeremy, looks up from the dough he's busily plaiting into something wonderful as I walk in the side entrance straight to the kitchen.

"Mornin' Miss G!" Jeremy waves, turning to give something bubbling away on the stove a stir before returning to the dough.

"Good morning," I smile, crossing the kitchen to my tiny office and grabbing an apron off the hook. Tying it at my waist, I move around the shop, getting ready to open for the day. As I move through my usual routine, my mind has time to wander back to the invitation. I wonder how much thought she put into sending it to me. I wonder if she'd sincerely like me to be there for her day, or if she feels an obligation to honor the friendship we had before I fucked it all up.

A tentative tap on the glass window of the front door yanks me out of my musings. Startling, I glance at the clock, muttering a curse under my breath when I realize I've daydreamed my way to three minutes past seven. Quickly walking to the door, I flip the little sign to 'open', throw the bolt and open the door, smiling at the woman standing just outside in the morning sun.

"Sorry about that, lost the time for a moment," I step back and wave her in with a smile. "Welcome to Perky." She's wearing crisp blue scrubs and she's got long brown hair in a sleek ponytail that hangs midway down her back.

"No worries, sorry if I startled you," her smile reveals perfect white teeth and dimples. Her southern drawl is light and cultured. *I'm kind of instantly obsessed.* Walking quickly behind the counter, I give her a moment to look over the menu board.

"Hmmm, I'll take a plain cappuccino, the biggest one you make," she pauses, looking over the baked goods in the glass case, "and one of those vanilla bean scones."

"Excellent choice," I slide the back of the case open to get her scone, "Jeremy just baked those last night, they are *divine*."

"Divine sounds perfect, thanks," she smiles. There's a buzzing from her pocket, she pulls out her phone and taps the screen, stepping away from the counter.

"Dr. Nichols," she says crisply into the phone, shifting her bag higher on her shoulder. While she's talking, I carefully put the scone in a small paper bag and make her cappuccino. She appears to be listening as she turns back to the counter, mutely handing me a twenty.

"Joanie, tell her I'll be there in five, this is getting ridiculous," she sighs, disconnecting. Taking the change I hold out, she tucks it in a pocket of her bag before reaching for the small bag with her scone inside and her coffee.

"Thanks, I need this, it's shaping up to be a hell of a day already," she sighs with a small smile.

Thanks for stopping by and good luck, I hope it turns around," we smile at each other for a second and then she's out the door and gone.

Coffee Fix Found

J enna

Ohmygod that coffee shop was a find. I've already decided it's now my coffee place. The scone was melt-in-my-mouth perfect and the cappuccino was rich and delicious. Plus the name, Perky, is freaking adorable.

Moving has been tough, but I'm finally feeling settled in, starting to explore a little. There's a beautiful historic district here, with tons of little boutiques and restaurants. I just stumbled across Perky this morning and it's right around the corner from the apartment I'm renting.

Brushing crumbs off my scrub top, I pick up the pace, quickly walking the remaining three blocks to the clinic. I've got an anxious mother in the waiting room already.

It's game on when I walk in the door. I'm the newest physician for Community Health. There are a lot of walk-ins. Dropping my bag in my locker, I wash my hands and head for the central desk. From there it's a shit-show for almost ten hours, with a twenty minute break for lunch that I eat standing up while I dictate. The crazy thing? I love every minute of it, the pace, the different cases, helping people, it's my thing.

I'm dragging by the time I get back to my apartment, tossing a pile of mail on the table and eating a slice of cold pizza straight out of the fridge. After standing in the shower for a solid twenty minutes letting the water pound the knots out of my shoulders I feel human again.

Pulling on yoga pants and my favorite baggy sweatshirt, I curl up on the couch and decide to binge a baking show for a couple of hours. It's lonely in the city, but I know I've got to give it some time, I've only been here a few weeks. *Hey, at least I can check 'find my new coffee house' off the list of things that will make me love it here.*

Maybe someday soon I'll break down and go see if there are any cats at the animal shelter that I need to bring home. I've been wanting to adopt one ever since I was a cat-sitter for a friend back in Texas once.

Max was such a love, he was a beautiful black ball of purrs and now I miss having a cat around. I didn't let myself adopt one while I was doing my residency, the hours were just too crazy for me to be responsible for anything. Now that I'm settling in and my hours are a lot more regular, I think I would probably make a good cat-mom.

Pausing the show, I walk into the kitchen and grab another slice of pizza and pour myself a glass of merlot. *Yep, I think I'm a cat-mom in the making.* My mind wanders to the owner of the coffee shop. I wonder what her name is...

What a Week

*G*abrielle

On Tuesday, the doctor with brown eyes and shiny hair ordered a cappuccino and a blueberry muffin. Wednesday, I decided her eyes were really more of a hazel and she ordered cappuccino and blackberry tartlet. By Thursday, I made a joke about her being a regular now, *that was pretty well received*, she ordered cappuccino and a piece of carrot cake.

On Friday, she told me her name is Jenna. Granted, it was because the shop was slammed and I was writing names on cups so that my barista Kellie could keep things straight, but she told me.

On Saturday we had our first conversation.

"Oh I'm a Texas girl," Jenna laughed, when I asked her where she was from originally. "How about you?" Jenna is sitting at one of the little tables near the window. She arrived around nine this morning, looking different in street clothes rather than her usual blue scrubs.

"Miami, actually," I grin, "Mama fell in love and let my dad haul her all over the country. Most of his family was from around here, so I've always had a soft spot."

"I can see why," Jenna nods, "it's beautiful here, the architecture downtown is so well preserved. I love this building, by the way, it's amazing."

"Oh, thank you, it's been quite a labor of love. This used to be my uncle's coin shop," I lean a hip against her table and look around, remembering. "It had a number of unfortunate renovations in the 80's that had to be undone, but I'm really happy with how everything turned out."

"Well you've removed all traces of the 80's, that's for certain," Jenna smiles looking around at the rich wooden floors and exposed brick and beams. "I love the old industrial look, so strong and clean, but a little imperfect too, you know?" I feel a little flutter of excitement in my stomach. That's exactly what I love about this place, I'm so proud of the space I've created.

Just then, a small herd of teenagers come bubbling through the door. I squelch a sigh of regret because I'd rather stay here, talking to Jenna.

"Duty calls," I joke, reaching over to take her empty plate to the counter with me. "It was nice talking with you, Jenna."

"Good luck," she grins, "I'll see you later, Gabrielle."

Jenna opens her book and reads while she finishes her coffee. The girls were just the beginning of the Saturday rush. I'm busily running my tail off when she heads out the door with a wave.

It makes me smile every morning when Jenna walks through the door. I usually take Sunday and Monday as my days off. This week, I find myself thinking of reasons to head downstairs

136

and check in on the shop.

On Thursday, Jenna walks through the door holding a flyer printed on bright yellow paper. She hands it to me with a smile as she looks over the baked goods for her daily treat.

The flyer is advertising a historical architecture walk that is going to take place in the center of the city this Saturday afternoon. It's the area where the courthouse and other government buildings stand.

"After we talked on Saturday, I saw this poster on a bulletin board at my Chinese take out place," Jenna smiles, "I was wondering if you'd like to go with me?" My stomach does a little flip.

"I'd love to," I hand Jenna her cappuccino. Her smile broadens.

"Great! Do you want to meet here around three?" She waits for me to agree and then chooses a brownie.

Rainy Date

J enna

Saturday dawns overcast and dreary. Normally I enjoy the rain, but I'm going to be bummed if it ruins the first plans I've made with another human since I arrived. Checking the weather, it looks like the rain will come later on tonight. Hopefully the walk will happen as scheduled. I throw a tiny travel umbrella in my bag, just in case and go dig up the flyer. In small letters at the bottom it says: rain or shine.

I'm looking forward to spending time with Gabrielle outside of the coffee shop. It's a beautiful shop, the coffee and bakery are amazing, but there's always the little aura of being served that hangs over us. I want to get to know her, she's smart and interesting…beautiful.

When I walked into her coffee shop over a week ago, Gabrielle took my breath away. She was wearing a pink t-shirt with a black apron over it, jeans and little black flats. Her brown skin has a rich golden tone, her brown eyes dance when she smiles. She wears her dark hair in natural ringlets that bounce when she moves.

I've been a smitten kitten since, looking for a way to ask Gabrielle on a date. From the way she acts when I walk in the door each morning, I'm pretty sure Gabrielle likes me too.

* * *

Forcing myself to get some laundry done and clean my apartment, the day passes fairly quickly. The rain holds off, as promised, even allowing the sun to break through periodically.

Pulling on dark jeans, a black tank and a light grey sweater with a large neckline that falls off my shoulder, I glance in the mirror. Swiping on some mascara, I pull my hair up into a loose chignon and put in some dangly silver earrings.

Stepping into a cute pair of short rain boots I bought months ago and have never had a chance to wear, I grab my bag and walk out the door. I'm excited and nervous as I walk the two blocks to Gabrielle's coffee shop.

"Hey, you look great," Gabrielle sets aside some receipts she's looking over and walks around the counter to meet me.

"Thanks, so do you, I'm glad you got the memo that it might rain," I laugh. Gabrielle is wearing short rain boots in an almost identical style to mine, but where mine are a fairly muted gray plaid pattern, hers are bright red. She's wearing a short denim skirt and a red sweater.

"Right?" Gabrielle grins, "I've been looking for an opportunity to wear these, they're so cute, but weirdly impractical." Walking to the end of the counter, she reaches to a lower shelf and shoulders a brown leather hobo bag.

"Shall we?"

Cozy is Good

***

*G*abrielle

"To top it all off, I shit you not, the woman looked right at me and said she couldn't be pregnant, she'd only let her boyfriend, *and I quote*, "bump her rump,"" Jenna laughs, reaching for the wine and refilling mine before she pours herself another.

"Ohmygod, okay, that's it, you win," I laugh, reaching over and clinking the edge of my glass to hers. "Cheers to crazy shit that happens at work."

"I'll drink to that, Darlin'," Jenna laughs with me, "in fact, I sometimes drink *because* of that."

The walk was really interesting. Jenna and I agreed that the history of some of the buildings was unexpected, and the guide really made an effort to toss us some 'off the beaten path' trivia and stories that were fascinating. Afterwards, we were both starving and Jenna suggested dinner.

The conversation, *and the wine*, have been flowing smoothly and I can't remember the last time I had so much fun. We've been sitting in Jenna's 'Italian place', a lovely little Italian bistro called Olive's for a couple of hours. The gnocchi with handmade meatballs is *amazing*.

"So," I pause to take a bite *because I can't stop shovelling this food in my mouth*, "this is your Italian place," Jenna nods, "and you mentioned you found the flyer at your 'Chinese place'," Jenna nods again. "Do you have other places?" I ask, grinning. Jenna swallows her bite and laughs.

"Yeah, I always sound crazy when this comes up, but I don't do…change…well." Jenna smiles, stirring the food around on her plate. "When I live somewhere new, I try restaurants until I find my favorite thing in that style of food. Once I find my favorite thing, that's my place." She shrugs, embarrassed, "I came to Olive's and ate the most amazing mushroom risotto I've ever had, so, Olive's is my Italian place."

"So do you ever eat at any other Italian places?" I wonder out loud.

"Only under duress," Jenna laughs, "or if the food suddenly changes and I need to find a new place."

"So, what's your 'Chinese place'?"

"Golden Noodle, Bangkok beef," she smiles.

"Indian?"

"Taj Maj, Vegetable Korma."

"How many other places do you have?" I laugh, reaching for my wine.

"Welllll, Pizza, Burgers, French for when I feel fancy, Wings, Mexican, Greek," Jenna ticks them off on her fingers, "and of course, Perky, my coffeehouse," she finishes, giving me a wink.

* * *

When the bottle is long gone and the staff is cleaning around us, we leave the restaurant. The rain that has held off all day and into the night finally arrives, and as the first large drops fall, we duck into a doorway laughing. Jenna digs a tiny umbrella out of her bag.

"We can share, it'll be cozy," she offers, looking up at me as she opens the umbrella. *I love this plan.*

"Cozy works," I step close, tucking my bag at the back of my shoulder and sliding an arm around her shoulders. She's several inches shorter than I am and when she puts her arm around my waist, she's perfectly tucked into my side. We walk back to Perky, rain tapping gently on the umbrella, our rain boots splashing lightly through the puddles.

"This was really fun," We reach the awning outside Perky and Jenna lowers the umbrella, turning to face me. I feel a little pang of need as her arm leaves my waist.

"Agreed. We should definitely do this again," Jenna smiles, stepping closer to me, she reaches out and her fingers stroke lightly down my arm and then link with mine. We stare at each other a moment, our breaths just barely visible in the cool night air.

Finally, I gather my nerve and lean in, my lips brushing hers softly. Her fingers in mine pull me closer and I kiss her again, harder this time, our lips pressing together as I feel her hand cupping my jaw. When we finally step apart, she runs her thumb lightly over my lower lip, smiling.

"Goodnight, Gabrielle," she whispers.

"Goodnight, Jenna," I smile as she turns and walks away. I

unlock the door and float up the stairs to my apartment.

Taste Tester and Storyteller

*J*enna

Waking up the next morning, I go for a quick run and then text Gabrielle.

Me: Hey, what are you doing today?

Gabrielle: Hi, I'm at the shop now, we got a huge cinnamon roll order so I'm helping Jeremy get them ready. After that no plans. Want to come and taste test?

Me: taste test cinnamon rolls? I'm already out the door

Gabrielle: LOL ok see you soon

Showering quickly, I loosely braid my hair and pull on jeans and a soft yellow t-shirt. Grabbing my bag and my favorite wine-colored cardigan, I step into some flats and walk out the door.

The bell over the door jingles when I enter the shop and

Kellie, Gabrielle's barista greets me with a cappuccino.

"Gabrielle and Jeremy are in the kitchen, she said to send you on back," Kellie smiles, pointing to a short hallway to the left of the counter.

The kitchen smells so good I never want to leave. Gabrielle is stirring what looks like cinnamon roll filling in a large stainless bowl. She flashes me a bright smile as I walk through the doors.

"Hey you made it! Jenna this is Jeremy, baker extraordinaire," she gestures like a game show girl at a stocky man with white blonde hair and pale blue eyes. He's busily kneading a ball of dough and his hands never stop moving as he smiles at me.

"I'd shake your hand, but…" he laughs, "nice to meet you, Jenna."

"Oh no worries," I laugh, "I'd rather watch you bake. I've been enjoying all the amazing fruits of your labor for days now."

"Here's a front row seat," Gabrielle sets a stool next to me and squeezes my hand before returning to her bowl.

"Oh geez," I groan, "I feel spoiled, is there anything I can do to help?" Gabrielle giggles, glancing at Jeremy.

"Well, don't be mad, but I told Jeremy about all of your 'places' and we were kind of thinking that a list like that might indicate that you don't cook, or bake…at all." Her eyes are teasing and I burst out laughing.

"Ok, busted, I'll watch." I settle on the stool and sip the cappuccino, sighing appreciatively as I watch them move around the kitchen with easy familiarity. A few minutes later, a timer starts beeping. Jeremy moves to the oven, pulling out a large sheet of cinnamon rolls and setting them on a rack to begin cooling. He checks another sheet that has been cooling for a little while.

"These are ready to frost, Miss G," Jeremy turns back to the rolls he's building.

"On it," Gabrielle walks over to another counter, pulling cling wrap off of a bowl of frosting.

"Buttercream, buttercream, buttercream," she sings, as she finds a frosting knife and carefully tops off the rolls. When she's done, Gabrielle carefully cuts one free of the others and puts it on a plate, setting it in front of me with a smile.

"You go on, Miss G," Jeremy smiles, "I've got the rest."

"Ohhh, remind me to give you a raise sometime," Gabrielle laughs, patting his shoulder as she dishes up another roll.

"Jenna, I'll get a coffee and we can take these upstairs?"

"Okie-dokie," *eye roll, okie-dokie? Cheesy much?* I pick up my coffee and plate, following her out of the kitchen. We pause while Gabrielle makes a latte, then she takes me to a side door that leads to a stairwell running up the side of the building. The stairs are narrow and steep, but at the landing Gabrielle unlocks a heavy wooden door and opens it, waving me in.

Gabrielle lives in an open loft full of rich wood, bookshelves overflowing with books and plants on every flat surface. We come in close to the back of the building, there's a little entry hall with a laundry and bathroom off to either side. The hallway opens into a beautiful kitchen, concrete counters, farmhouse sink, open shelves, it's amazing. Beyond that is the living room, a bedroom and an office space. I'm silent as I look around, taking it all in.

"I get my green thumb from my Grandma and my bookworm tendencies from my Dad," Gabrielle offers shyly. I turn back to her, smiling.

"I'm jealous of both, this is *amazing*," walking further into the kitchen, there's a nook with a table. I set my coffee and cinnamon roll on it and pull out a chair.

"Later I'll show you the garden on the roof, it's one of my favorite spots, but it's hot this time of day," Gabrielle joins me at the table. Her laptop is sitting open, a search page full of flights on the screen.

"Taking a trip?"   *That's not completely nosy...whatever.* Gabrielle glances at the computer with a tiny frown.

"Sorry, none of my business," I pick up my coffee, embarrassed.

"No, no, it's not that, it's just...yes I'm thinking about a trip, but I don't know if I'm ready." Gabrielle explains. Playing with the cup in her hands, she sighs.

"My best friend Laurel is getting married in the Caribbean," she begins slowly, "but it's...complicated."

The Levels of Awkward

---

*G*abrielle

I tell Jenna the entire story, I don't leave anything out, including what a bitch I was when Laurel came to see me a few months ago while she packed up the last of her apartment stuff. Jenna is quiet, letting me get it all out, her eyes understanding.

"So…that's the long, awful story of how I ruined everything," I huff out a sigh, looking at Jenna.

"Well, I'm going to just point out that she *did* invite you to the wedding, so you haven't ruined *everything*," Jenna reaches across the table, taking one of my hands in hers. "A friendship like that isn't over just because you have a bad fight, Gabrielle. You guys just need to find your new normal. You need to give Laurel a chance to be around you. Her knowing that you had romantic feelings for her is going to take a beat to get used to, you know?"

"I know," I whisper, "there are just so many levels of awkward going on…I slept with her boyfriend, which definitely doesn't send the 'hey I'm into women' signal. I got drunk and unloaded *that* gem on her when she wasn't expecting it. Top that off with insisting that she 'try' liking me back and I'm pretty much the biggest jackass ever." I bury my face in my hands, Jenna laughs softly.

"Well, when you do something you don't hold back a thing, that's for sure, but your passion is a part of who you are, she's known you for a long time." Jenna stands, taking my hands and pulling me up out of my chair. "Take this for the olive branch that it is, your friend wants you to be at her wedding." Jenna says firmly. I stare at her for a long moment.

"Okay," I whisper, reaching for her and closing the distance. Jenna's hands slide around my waist as I cup her face in both hands, kissing her hard. I feel her tongue flick across my lips and open to her, deepening the kiss. When we finally take a breath, we stand there for a while, foreheads pressed together.

"I don't suppose there's any chance you want to be my plus one?" I ask lightly, Jenna giggles.

"Darlin', as much as you and I on a Caribbean vacation sounds amazing," she kisses me again, lightly, "I think that would send the wrong signal. You two need to patch things up first. She needs to know that you dating me has nothing to do with her, if I go it's too complicated." *She said we're dating. I really like the sound of that, a lot.*

"Mmmph," I grumble, "you're right. I don't like it, but you're right." I reach for her again, pulling her into a hug. "Thank you."

"I'll be right here, waiting for you when you get back," Jenna whispers.

Black and White Things

*J*enna

The next two weeks fly by, I stop in every day for my morning coffee and to see Gabrielle before I go to the clinic. In the evenings we have dinner and spend time together, usually on the roof garden. It's a magical space full of plants and twinkle lights. We lay on a huge lounge chair built for two and look at the stars. Most nights I sleep in her bed, waking up to her lips on my skin.

Today, when I leave the clinic, I find Gabrielle waiting on a bench outside the doors. She stands quickly, her curls bouncing on her shoulders when she sees me.

"Hey, I've got a surprise, want to take a ride?" Gabrielle's eyes are gleaming with excitement. *I loathe surprises...but I really like her, so let's do whatever this is.*

"Okay," I laugh, walking over and kissing her hello. Gabrielle drives us across town and my stomach gives a little flutter of happiness when she pulls into the parking lot of the city Animal Control center. She turns to me, smiling.

"So…ever since you told me about Max, I've been stalking their website," Gabrielle laughs nervously, "and there are a pair of dumpster kittens that arrived this morning that I think you might want to meet."

"Ohmygod." I'm out of the car and she laughs as I turn, waiting impatiently.

"I'll take that as a yes." Gabrielle catches up to me, linking her arm through mine.

An hour later, after a little paperwork and Gabrielle's credit card being run through, *she was so sweet, being all sneaky while I was cuddling the furbabies,* we walk back to the car with a cat carrier holding two sleeping kittens. Both are females, both black and white and utterly perfect.

"They are so stinking cute," I whisper, opening the top of the box to stroke one sleepy kitten's head. The kitten immediately goes belly up, batting at my finger and then letting me rumple her fur.

"Have you thought about names? My only request is that they do not become Maxine and Maxette," Gabrielle laughs and I join her.

"Oh no, something cuter for this pair." I stare in the box, musing, "Black and white things…Salt and Pepper? Is that too cliche?"

"Probably, but in a really cute way, look at *us* after all," Gabrielle assures me with a smile, holding her arm next to mine. "See?"

"Well, I used to love to play chess with my brother, Rook and Bishop?"

"Also really good choices," she nods.

"Any thoughts on a fun coffee reference?" I tap my finger to my lip, thinking, "Mocha and Cappuccino seem too obvious…"

"Um…Breve, Leche, Doppio?" Gabrielle offers.

"What's a doppio? It sounds adorable."

"A double shot of espresso," she smiles. I stare down into the box for a minute, looking at the kittens, one of them is decidedly more white with black spots while the other has a strong black patch wrapping around her belly.

"Breve and Doppio. I love it."

After a stop at a pet supply store, we head to my apartment to get the kittens all set up. As Gabrielle pulls up to the curb, I realize it's the first time she's seen my place.

"Well there's no super cool roof garden, but it's home," I carefully close the box with the kittens inside, picking up a bag of cat food in my other hand. Gabrielle looks up at the building, smiling.

"It's very modern, cool…I can see why you like it," she says carefully, glancing at me.

"Oh, it's just a place to live, but thanks for being nice," I laugh, thinking about the beautiful historical details of her loft.

"So if I talk you into moving in with me, there won't be an argument about which place?" Gabrielle's laugh cuts off in a strangled wheeze and her eyes widen. "I mean, you know, someday, I haven't been thinking about it, I mean we umm… fhoooooo." she gives up and blows out a big breath.

"No argument at all," I tease. Walking up close in spite of the load I'm carrying, I turn my face up to hers, "kiss me before you hurt yourself." Gabrielle laughs and leans in, pressing her lips to mine. Leaning back just enough to look in my eyes, she takes a deep breath.

"What if I asked you now?" Gabrielle whispers. My heart stutters and then returns to normal. *Can't say I haven't been thinking about it every night since I met her...well I could, but I would be lying.*

"I'd say yes," I whisper back. Her lips crash back into mine, her hand slides down my arm, gently taking the bag of cat food. She breaks the kiss with a brilliant smile.

"Let's go home."

Love is Love is Love

*G*abrielle

The morning of Laurel's wedding dawns clear and
perfect. I arrived yesterday afternoon. Margo arranged
for me to have one of the rooms in a tiny mom-n-pop hotel
that she booked for family and friends. *Of course, prior to that, I
had to promise Margo that I was not in fact coming to cause any sort
of trouble. Margo, in turn, promised me death by fonging if I did
cause a scene. Now I'm mostly curious about this movie reference,
I'll have to tell Jenna to put it on our list of 'must see'.*

I haven't seen Laurel yet, I didn't want to crash the rehearsal,
but Margo invited me to breakfast, *insert more stern warnings
not to upset the bride,* at her home this morning. As I walk up the
steps I mentally cringe, thinking of the terrible conversation I
had with Laurel the last time I was in this house. Squaring my
shoulders, I ring the bell.

Williams answers, his stern face breaking into a cautious

smile.

"Good morning, Gabrielle," he steps back, ushering me into the entryway. "Laurel is on the deck off the kitchen, I trust you remember the way?" When I nod, he gives me another small smile and walks the opposite direction to his office, closing the door softly. I walk down a short hall, coming into the back side of the kitchen and crossing to the deck. Laurel is sitting at the table, picking at a muffin, her eyes on the ocean.

"You should probably eat that," I tease lightly, "you've got a big day ahead of you." Laurel turns, standing quickly and walks over to me. Without a pause, her arms wrap around me as she hugs me, hard.

"Gabs, you made it!" Laurel leans back, still holding my arms, "I'm so glad you came."

"I'm so glad you invited me," my voice is thin, nervous. I take a deep breath and try again. "I want you to know how sorry I am. Nothing I put you through was fair." Laurel starts shaking her head, tears in her eyes. "Please, let me finish," I beg. "I just want you to know that if you'll have me as your friend again, that will *always* be enough. I was confused and trying to figure myself out. You've always been my rock, Laurel, and somewhere along the way I thought our friendship was turning into something it wasn't. Forgive me."

"Of course I do," Laurel pulls me into a bone-crushing hug, I can feel it right to my soul and it feels good.

* * *

Laurel and I talk and laugh until Margo comes to tell Laurel it's time for her to see the hair stylist. Margo smiles at us both, patting me on the shoulder.

"I'm glad to see you two so happy, it's a wedding, everyone is *going* to be happy!" She mock finger-wags us as we laugh. Laurel and I stand and I give her another hug.

"I'll see you later, I'm so happy for you and Trey," I whisper.

"Thanks, I hope someday soon I can meet the person who's putting the bounce in *your* step," Laurel whispers back. I stare at her for a minute, I haven't mentioned Jenna yet.

"Oh for fuckssake," Laurel laughs, "we've been friends for *twenty years*, Gabs." I burst out laughing.

"I love you, my friend," we beam at each other, still giggling.

"I love you back, my friend."

* * *

Heading back to the hotel, I shower and then lounge around in my robe, not wanting to wrinkle my dress before the wedding. While I'm flipping through the options on the antiquated TV, my phone starts pinging for a video chat. My heart beats a little faster when Jenna's beautiful face fills the screen.

"Oops, too close," she laughs, moving away a little bit and waving at me.

"I miss you," I smile.

"I miss you," Jenna smiles back. "Did you get to talk to Laurel?"

"I did," I nod, smiling. "We're good. I feel really good, it was the right thing to do, coming to the wedding."

"Oh, that's awesome! Now are you *sure* you don't want to take a couple extra days? You're in the islands, baby!" Jenna bubbles, excited. I shrug, laughing.

157

"Nah, I'll be home late tomorrow. Everything I need is at home."

"Awww, you always know what to say." Jenna leans out of frame and then sits back up, holding Doppio. "These little babies miss you too." We both laugh as Doppio crawls right onto the table, nosing the camera. "Okay, I won't keep you, tell me all about the wedding when you get home, okay? Call me from the airport?"

"I will," I affirm, "see you soon." *That doesn't feel like enough.* "Jenna?"

"Yes, Darlin'?" she smiles.

"I love you." *That feels so right.*

"Oh Darlin', I love you too." With a brilliant smile, she disconnects.

* * *

The wedding takes place about an hour before sunset. Margo is running around, flawlessly pulling everything together as I arrive at her bar.

"Hey Gabs, you can ride with me, everything is set for the reception later, so it's time for me to get to the wedding too." She rushes by, waving for me to keep up.

"Oh, is the wedding on another beach?" I ask, surprised, I kind of assumed the wedding would be on the beach right outside Margo's place.

"No, no, no," Margo laughs, "this is no ordinary beach wedding, girlfriend, hop in." Margo has a golf cart waiting for her at the side of the bar. There are several golf carts lined up on the road and as guests arrive, they are loaded into the golf carts and off they go. I climb in and hold on as she floors it, listening to the little engine whine.

After a beautiful drive over rolling hills towards the center of the island, she slows, turning onto a path marked by roughly two million twinkle lights and ribbons in every shade of blue. The trees canopy over the path, and the entire thing is lit until it opens to a clearing. I gasp out loud, it's amazing.

"That's the reaction I was hoping for, Gabs," Margo laughs.

"Ohmygod, Margo, I can't even, I have no words for how beautiful this place is, no words." I climb out of the golf cart and look around in wonder.

There is a pool in the middle of the clearing, the water a bright, clear blue. At the far end is a waterfall, opposite it there's a gap in the rocks that the water runs through. To either side of the path we drove in on, there are white chairs for guests, circling half of the pool, filling the grassy area in front of the trees. Twinkle lights fill the trees behind the chairs.

In the middle of the pool is a large, flat rock. Directly in front of the path we drove in on, a simple white bridge spans the water between the shore and the flat rock. An archway full of flowers in shades of pink and gold stands on the rock. I can smell the flower's perfume on the light breeze.

"Margo, this is epically perfect," I can't stop looking around. *I wish Jenna were here to see this, ohmygod.* Margo gives me a one-armed hug, holding tightly to her ever-present tablet.

"Thanks sweetie. Your seat is over there, I'll see you after, okay?" Margo hands me off to an usher who holds out his arm and helps me to a seat in the front row up the side closer to the waterfall. I wave at friends and family as they are seated, my head still on a swivel as I try to take it all in.

Everyone quiets when a string quartet starts playing from

somewhere across the pool. The minister walks across the bridge, standing under the archway. I see Margo take her seat just off the aisle in the front row.

We all turn as the music changes and Trey walks his mother up the aisle, his father right behind them. She's already tearful, but smiling brightly as he hugs her and then he crosses the bridge and turns to wait for Laurel. His pants are smoky blue, his shirt a cream linen with the sleeves loosely cuffed. He has a tiny wreath of pink and gold flowers around one wrist.

The music changes again. Everyone turns to look as Laurel appears, walking with her father. She is radiant with happiness. Her vibrant hair is half up, loose braids shaping it into a crown with the rest falling in loose waves down her back. A gossamer thin veil flutters behind her, the edge lined with tiny crystals that glimmer in the light.

Laurel's dress just barely skims the ground as she walks. The thinnest of straps cross her shoulders, holding up a vintage lace bohemian confection. Hugging her body to the hips, it flows to the ground, swaying gracefully, her little gold flats peeking out with every step. She's got a tiny wreath to match Trey's on one wrist.

Williams is in light tan and blue linen. His face is serious, eyes bright, as he walks with Laurel on his arm. Trey crosses the bridge to meet them as Williams gives Laurel a careful hug and places her hand in Trey's. He shakes Trey's hand, leaning in to whisper something to Trey that makes all three of them smile. Williams moves to sit by Margo, putting an arm around her, as Trey and Laurel cross the bridge together to stand before the minister.

The music fades and the ceremony begins, the minister's gentle cadence rolling over the crowd assembled to watch

Laurel and Trey exchange vows. Eventually he pauses, looking expectantly at Laurel. She joins hands with Trey.

"Trey, I've looked back at our time together and all I can feel is thankful for everything that brought me to *that* beach on *that* day," her voice is clear in the silence. "I feel the most perfect balance and contentment when I am with you. I promise to love, respect and incessantly photograph you," she smiles teasingly as a ripple of laughter rolls through the crowd, "for the rest of my life."

The minister smiles, nodding at Trey to begin.

"Laurel, one time you told me that when we are together it felt like the sun was shining just for you. I've never been able to come up with better words to describe how you make me feel. I will love, respect and never laugh when you try to get in a hammock, for the rest of my life." Another little ripple of laughter rolls through the crowd as Laurel and Trey beam at each other happily.

The minister steps forward and Laurel and Trey exchange rings. As expected, Margo's timing proves to be impeccable. The couple is presented to the crowd and Trey is given permission to kiss his bride. Trey takes Laurel's face gently between his hands and her arms slide around his waist. He kisses her as the sun sets behind them and there is not a dry eye in the crowd.

* * *

Thanks for reading! If you want more, here's a little teaser.

Crystal, the drunken tarot card reader from Las Vegas, *you met her in Finding My Safe*, has a story of her own…Finding My Cards, coming soon.

~~~~~

Crystal

My man died.

Fucker fell and hit his fucking head on some steps coming out of a bar, and here I am, alone. Wine helps. He wasn't much of a man…he never got over his dead wife and I was a distant second, but it was nice having someone…not being alone…

I'm not sure when I last put some clothes on, but the smell tells me I need to shower. Glancing around the room, I feel like I'm in a fishbowl. Everything's blurry and feels thick…slow. Maybe I'm sober for the first time in months, I don't know.

"Get up, Woman." A man's voice rumbles from across the

room.

I turn my head, slow-like so the room doesn't tilt, and see him standing in the damn doorway like he owns the place.

"Fuck off Cal." The words whisper out with the promise to my stomach that I'll let it barf if it can give me ten seconds to find the shitter. He laughs as I sit up and find my feet, staggering across the room that doesn't feel quite level, grabbing the smooth porcelain and offering up everything I ever ate.

"I repeat...fuck off Cal," I whisper, wishing it was a scream.

Time to Poke the Bear

Cal

She's stumbling around, sniping at me as she finds a pair of jeans on the floor. Lifting one foot to thread into the leg of the jeans, she tips over with an offended shriek, landing on the bed.

"Stop laughing you jackass!" Crystal's finally angry enough to breathe fire. *That's good, that's what it will take to get her moving.*

"You don't need jeans yet anyway," I reach over and pull them out of her hands as she tries to put them on while she's flat on her back on the bed. She kicks her legs anyway, pissed.

"You look like a dyin' bug doin' that." I sniff dramatically, waving a hand in front of my face. "You're taking a bath."

"The fuck I am!" She shrieks again as I grab her ankles and yank her towards the edge of the bed. Ignoring her hands swatting at my head and shoulders I scoop her up and stomp towards the bathroom. *She feels too skinny. I wonder when she ate last.*

"Knock it off, Woman," I grunt as she lands an elbow in my ribs. Tightening my grip I give her a shake. "Do that again and I'll drop your ass on the floor. You smell like a damn dog that rolled in a skunk carcass."

Ignoring her outraged screech, I kick the door shut behind us and let go of Crystal's legs, keeping one arm around her waist so she doesn't *actually* fall on her ass while I turn on the water. She looks surprised to be on her feet, and even more surprised when I shove her in the shower still wearing her t-shirt and underwear.

"Eeeeaaaaaaah! It's freezing!" Crystal howls as I hide a grin and yank the curtain shut. I hear her fumbling with the controls, but she doesn't shut off the water. Finally her squeals turn into grumbling.

I hear a wet slap, followed by another, as she peels off her clothes and drops them on the floor of the shower. As steam starts to fill the tiny bathroom, I watch her silhouette for a moment. Crystal tilts back her head, wetting her long, black hair and I hear a tiny sigh of pleasure escape her lips. Turning, I walk out to the living room, giving her some space.

Grabbing one of the boxes I left by the door when I walked in, I look around the room. Crappy furniture can stay here, but I grab a sweater hanging over a chair and wrap up the three framed pictures on the tiny little mantle. Putting them in the box, I do the same with the contents of the side table drawer and a beat up desk. All the books and a battered photo album from a small shelf under the window fill up another box. I walk out and load the boxes into my truck, grabbing more boxes as I head back in the house.

I can still hear the shower running, so I head for the kitchen. A small table and chair takes up the middle, a throwback to the fifties that gleams compared to the rest of the room. I know it was her grandma's, so I carry it outside. Tossing a blanket in the truck I put it in upside down and add the chairs. Most of her dishes are mismatched junk, but I rifle through the cupboards to see if she's got her Ma's stuff tucked anywhere. Nothing but chipped ceramic and plastic bar cups until I open the cupboard up over the fridge.

The ceiling light shines off an old copper tea kettle. There are several tea cups, all different patterns but definitely special, with the little saucers to match. I look over at the stove and there's a beat up tin kettle on the burner, but this copper one sat on her ma's stove for years. Pulling open drawers, I find the dish towels and wrap up the cups and saucers, boxing them all up along with the kettle.

As I clear the shelf, my fingers bump a metal box. Taking it down, I open it and find a bag of weed inside. Shaking my head, I'm about to throw it away when Crystal walks into the kitchen.

"What are you doing, Cal?" She stops in the spot where her table used to be, looking confused. "Where the hell is my table?" Reaching out, she yanks the little box from my hands. Holding it protectively to her chest she takes a step back, flipping her dark hair off her shoulder.

"Dammit, Crystal," I ignore her questions, pointing at the box in her hands. "You don't need that shit." I wave a hand around the room and her eyes follow, taking in her dingy little kitchen. "Look what it does for you." I shrug, jamming my hands in my pockets as her eyes narrow.

"Judg-y much? You can fuck right off, Cal, this is TEA." She slams the box on the counter and grabs the tea pot off the stove, shoving it under the tap to fill with water. *Damn.*

"Easy mistake," I mutter, feeling stupid as she plants her hands on the counter, her back to me. Her head drops down and she sighs but doesn't say another word as we stand there.

The kettle whistling breaks the silence and Crystal pulls a battered mug off a shelf. Opening the box of tea, she gives me another narrow look as she spoons out the roughly cut leaves and adds the hot water. I smile reading her mug, it's got a tired looking gypsy cartoon with the caption, 'hang on, I gotta wake up my third eye', in faded type on the side.

"Get your own if you want," Crystal snaps, brushing past me with her tea. She doesn't see me grin, *because even pissed off she can't bring herself not to offer tea,* her shoulders stiff as she marches in and settles on the couch.

Glancing around I don't see anything else she'd want to hang on to from the kitchen, so I carry the boxes out and put them in the back of my truck. She eyes me over the rim of my mug as I walk back in and take a box to the bedroom. I ignore her, pulling open drawers and boxing up her things. Finally, curiosity gets the best of her and she clears her throat, leaning against the frame of the bedroom door.

"Why are you packing my shit, Cal?" She's trying to make her voice hard, but I look at her, hearing how tired she is, how alone.

About the Author

Halo Roberts is a writer of steamy rom-coms, lover of coffee and dark beer, and spoiler of two fat cats affectionately known as the Bitchy Betas. She's living happily ever after in Iowa with her very own hunky farm boy, and a small herd of stubborn mules that look a lot like children.

Head on over to haloroberts.com, sign up for Halo's newsletter and receive a free download of her short story, A Night at the Diner.

You can connect with me on:
- http://haloroberts.com
- https://twitter.com/RobertsHalo
- https://www.facebook.com/halorobertsauthor
- https://www.bookbub.com/profile/halo-roberts
- https://www.instagram.com/halorobertswrites
- http://bit.ly/halogoodreads

Subscribe to my newsletter:

✉ http://haloroberts.com

Also by Halo Roberts

Sweet, steamy, laugh-out-loud romantic comedies that always end in a happily ever after...or two.

Finding My Night
Second star to the right...

A sassy chef with a crush on her boss finds herself on a 'not-a-date' with him in this hilariously steamy romp. Complete with a problematic socialite, a cream puff fiasco, and a killer dress with a strategic peek of lace, there might also be a man-bun...a pair of dueling best friends...and a wedding...or two.

Finding My One
Blue skies and dirt roads and peaches, oh my...

A real job with the family business or goodbye trust fund...my parents have lost their minds. The icing on this craptastic cake is setting up headquarters in some backwater southern town, complete with a partner...a rugged, country, single dad that flips every switch I've got...and a few I didn't know about. ~Veronica

Things are heating up in the country...

Finding My Safe
The songs say love is in the water... and strange...

When chance brings Wren and Kane together again, things have changed. Wren is graduating med school, soon to start her residency. Kane is a bouncer at a crappy roadside bar. When an ambush in an alley makes him depend on Wren far more than he expected, can they find love in the midst of five-dollar tequila shots, surprise proposals and the bright lights of Las Vegas?

Here's hoping love is also at Joe's bar...and not actually strange.

Finding My Sun

Breakups suck.

They suck even more after you drunk-enly tell your A-list rock star boyfriend that you love him...then find your now ex best friend in his bed. Welcome to Laurel's world. So, what's a girl with a mangled heart to do? Escape to the Caribbean for some sun, sangria, and...a surfer?

Laurel meets Trey and sparks fly, hammocks flip, and all signs point to love. But when best friend and rock star drama invades the island, can new love last? Laurel has decisions to make, hearts to break and a sunburn to avoid in this two-part romantic comedy.